When in Tokyo

By Imani Lewis

When in Tokyo

Copyright © 2021 by Imani Lewis

Imani Lewis

Dedicated to my brand-new baby girl, Emery. I love you and you will always inspire me to go forward.

"I thought cherry blossoms bloom in the spring…
but with you around, they bloom anytime."

-    Rima Reyka

Prologue

Most people don't get to see the world until they're old and retired. Most people don't even leave the state they were born and raised in, not even for a funeral.

I wasn't most people though.

Unlike most people, I was granted the opportunity of a lifetime.

I was about to spend my summer in one of the most beautiful, high-paced, electrifying and enchanting cities in the world.

I, ladies and gentlemen, was going to Tokyo.

After graduating from the University of Pittsburgh with a degree in Social Science, I took a job as an intern *to* the intern of the research analyst at a company called *Inside the Mind.* This meant that I was running the intern's errands for her while she got the hands-on experience I craved.

I worked there for three months, barely making enough money to buy ramen noodle packets to keep me alive. My dad offered to pay my rent and bills until I was offered a real full-time position, but I turned him down. He was just able to get business booming again at the picture frame shop he owned in downtown Manhattan. He almost had to file for bankruptcy until he took one last chance and hired this girl he found selling art on the street. Apparently, her ideas for the shop caught the eyes of tourists and gave pops a newfound sense of "fame" if you will.

I couldn't burden him, especially when he just made it out the jaws of homelessness. Well, he wouldn't have been homeless seeing as my mom would've found a way to make some extra money. She was always coming up with new business ideas and schemes she wanted my dad to try. She didn't believe in giving up and never let anyone say the words "I can't".

About a month ago, my best friend, Theo, who I've known since I was in diapers, called me telling me how his new life in Tokyo was. He graduated from the University of Pittsburgh with me but got his degree in Liberal Arts. He was always obsessed with science and math growing up, exercising his brain muscles. I was more obsessed with figuring out why people were the way they were and why they make the decisions that they do.

Theo was offered a job straight out of college to a company in Tokyo I can't remember the name of, and he jumped at the opportunity, as he should have. I can't lie, I've missed him like crazy since he's been gone, but I know that he's securing his future and I'm happy that he gets to do what he loves.

So anyway, Theo called me last month talking about his job and the new food he tried, when he randomly threw in a question that caused me to drop everything I knew and prepare to fly across the globe.

"Hey, so my company just opened up a new research facility that'll focus on brain activity and the study of human interactions. They were asking me if I knew anyone who would be a good fit to start off as an intern for a year as they continue to develop this area of study. I may have casually slipped your name in there and now they want to meet you. Would you be down? I know you have that wonderfully high-paying job over there but…"

I was speechless and so shocked that I couldn't even twitch my eye. I sat on my bed, frozen as ice.

"Ari? I mean look, you don't have to stay long, just say yes to meeting with them. I promise you'll love them and being here in this city is a whole new feeling. Also, I miss you, very much, so it'll mean a lot to me if you at least just came to visit."

"Yes," I rush out on a breath before I'm frozen in place again from the shock that's coursing through my body in waves. "Of course I'm down."

"I figured you'd say that, so I told them to just schedule a meeting and that you'd be there. I'll text you the details in a second. See you in a month!"

The line goes dead, and I drop the phone from my hand, but my arm is still raised up as if I'm holding the phone to my ear.

I was going to Tokyo.

Ariana Marcelle McNally was doing something spontaneous for once in her boring, sheltered life.

Tokyo, here I come.

One

"Ari! Over here!"

I put my hand over my eyes to shield them from the sun as I squint and look in the direction of the familiar voice. As soon as I see the face I'm looking for, a huge grin slides its way into my features, and I start running towards it.

"Wait your bags!" The voice calls out to me in a laugh and I stop to turn around and go back for them. I pick my duffle bag off the ground and grab my suitcase then take off running again.

"Theo!" I call out as I jump into the arms of the person I would do anything for. He engulfs me into a warm embrace and I sink into him, letting our bodies morph together. I take in his musky pine scent and Degree for men cool rush deodorant. His biceps flex as he squeezes me tighter and kisses me on the crown of my head.

After a beat, we reluctantly pull back from one another and he chucks me under my chin. I swat his chest and we both laugh. I can't hide the tear that slides down my face. He wipes it with the back of his index finger then takes a step back.

"Hey baby girl."

"I didn't realize how much I missed you until now," I say to him as I watch him pick up my bags. My best friend was a tall 6'3 slim man with a jawline that could slice boulders in half. Compared to my 5'4, he was basically a living Greek God who's taken pity on the common human girl. His eyes were a brown that was so dark, they looked black if you didn't pay that much attention. He had lashes for days and his muscles were sculpted to perfection. He reminded me of a young Superman.

There was a time when we were 10 and we thought we liked each other just because we were such close friends. I suggested that we kissed to see if there was a spark between us, but as soon as our lips locked, we busted out laughing and fake gagging. We decided then on that this relationship was strictly platonic and ever since then we've never brought it up again.

Don't get me wrong, the man is gorgeous, but I just can't see past the fact that he's basically my brother.

"I realized how much I missed you the first day I left," he winks at me, opening his trunk with one hand while his other holds my suitcase.

"You only realized it because you were away from everything you were familiar with. You just missed being comfortable," I challenge him.

He rounds the car and opens the door on the left side, motioning for me to get in. I keep forgetting that in Tokyo, they drive on the opposite side than we do in America. I wonder how long it took Theo to get used to it.

Once I was inside, he closed my door then opened the door behind me to toss my duffle bag in the seat. He finally settled into the driver seat and refused to pull off until I had my seatbelt on. Once I was fastened and secured, we eased into traffic and he continued with our conversation.

"I realized I missed you when I didn't wake up to hearing your mammoth snores through the apartment walls." He chuckles and I shake my head in protest.

"Last time I checked, you were the one who had to wear a mouthguard to help with your snoring." I show all my teeth as I point to the top row, emphasizing where his mouthpiece would sit.

"That was a retainer dummy," he looks at me like I grew two heads, "It just happened to help with the snoring a little. You know you miss living with me."

"No, *you* wish you still lived with me. I bet you don't even eat homecooked meals anymore do you?"

Even though he doesn't respond, I already know the answer.

The drive to his apartment felt like it went by fast because we got lost in the conversation and catching up. Yes, we called each other almost every day, but it still wasn't the same as being face to face.

We pulled up to a 6-story apartment building with windows and balcony's all around it. It looked brand new and like it hasn't even been broken in yet. I gaze through the window up at the building as Theo parallel parks onto the street.

"It's gorgeous isn't it? Wait until you see the inside."

We take the elevator to the 6th floor, and Theo slips his keys into the door at the far right-end of the hallway. Once inside, the first thing that I notice is the view through the sliding glass doors straight ahead in the living room. They led out to the balcony, and I was dying to go sit on said balcony so I could look at the lights of Tokyo when they came on at night. His apartment wasn't fully furnished and honestly felt kind of plain.

There was a couch but no coffee table in the living room, the kitchen was one long strip of cabinet and countertop, with a white fridge in the corner. He had a small, round breakfast table that was fit for no more than two people, and a 50" flat screen mounted on his living room wall.

"This place is…. Wow," is all I manage to say, and he eyes me carefully.

"You don't like it." He says simply as he takes my bags into a room to the right of the kitchen.

"No…I do…it's just, it doesn't feel…." I move my hands around searching for the right word to describe what I'm feeling before I settle on "Homey."

He comes back in the living room, placing his hands on his hips and looking around. His eyes find mine again and we look at each other before bursting out laughing.

"You're right, this place is shit. The company is paying for it, and this was all the furniture they started me off with, minus that TV. I bought that so I could make it feel more like my spot. Wait until you see the bedroom."

I shake my head as I follow him back into the room he just came out of, revealing a lonely mattress sitting on the floor covered in a plain white comforter.

"Viola, my godly throne." He plops down onto the mattress on the ground, almost breaking something in the process.

There was literally nothing in his bedroom but a floor to ceiling window and a mattress that rested on the floor.

"How do you live like this?" I ask him rhetorically.

He throws a pillow at me and I throw it back with more force, giggling as I do. Apparently, my stomach thought the exchange was amusing too because she decided to outdo my giggle by letting out a long laugh that I'm sure woke up all of Japan.

"Someone's hungry," Theo pointed out like I didn't hear my own stomach growl. "Come on, I'll take you to my favorite place."

A little while later, we arrived at a place Theo dubbed "A healthy Japanese spot sent from heaven". The actual name of the restaurant was Nabezo Shinjuku Meiji Dori, and no, I still don't know how to pronounce it despite the many times Theo repeated it before giving up.

On the outside, the restaurant was placed on a busy street with endless foot traffic that was so bad, I had to hold on tight to Theo's hand so I wouldn't get lost. We also had to go up a few flights of stairs to get to the actual restaurant because it was placed on the 7th floor, hidden away from all the other stores around it.

The inside of the restaurant was like a whole other world because of how small, cozy and inviting it felt. The lighting was slightly dimmed, so it gave off a chill, relaxing ambience.

We sat at a booth towards the middle, by the array of vegetables they had placed in a buffet style. There was a hot plate in the middle of our table that Theo explained we used to cook our food with. I looked at the menu with wide doe eyes because I had no idea what it said or what I wanted. It was all in Japanese and the only thing I could read were the huge numbers sitting next to the different menu items.

"See anything you like?" Theo asked me with amusement in his voice.

I raised my head from the menu I looked over a dozen times, trying to study some of the pictures to get a sense of what it was trying to describe to me. He placed his fist over his mouth, suppressing the laugh that wanted so desperately to escape from his mouth.

"I'm sorry, the look on your face just reminds me of how I felt when I first moved here. Completely lost and confused as hell."

"Ha Ha," I say as I kick him lightly under the table, "I'll just get what you usually get."

"I always choose the all you can eat option for an hour and 40 minutes. That way, I can try multiple different combinations and indulge my taste buds in new flavors every time. Also, the vegetables here are so fresh, you'd think they were plucked directly from the root they grew out of, so I tend to grab a lot of those."

"Well what meats specifically are your favorite? And is the soup good?" I look at the few words on the menu I can actually read, but it doesn't do me any good because the descriptions are what's important.

"My favorite is the Shabu Shabu, and I'm a man with expensive taste buds, so I order the Japanese beef and pork."

I rub my chin more, making it seem like the decision I'm making is a difficult one.

"Alright, I'll have all of that you just said. With some water."

He nods and flags down a waiter to tell them our order.

"I've never eaten so much food in my life," I say rubbing my belly as we step back under the Tokyo night sky.

My belly looked as if I was 5 months pregnant, and the top button of my jeans refused to button. The street was a little less busy than when we stepped into the restaurant a couple of hours before, but still too busy to stray too far behind Theodore.

"Pick up the pace grandma," he called to me over his shoulder as I felt my food coma starting to take over my body.

"I can't walk any faster than this. That pistachio ice cream really did a number on me." I call back but with half the amount of energy he gave me.

"Didn't I tell you it was perfect?" He slowed his pace down so we were now walking side by side.

"Yea, but you failed to mention the fact that I'd succumb to an almost vegetative state by the end of it all."

He throws his head back and laughs, causing a few of the women in the vicinity to turn their heads and stare at him longingly. I smirk at the affect he has on women, and the death stares they gave me when they realized I'm the one that made him release the sound they found seductive.

Humans are so lust-filled it's crazy.

Theo nudges my arm with his elbow, and I nudge him back.

"Want me to carry you the rest of the way? We still have a little bit of a ways to walk."

I shake my head in protest. "No, I'll be okay. Besides, you might drop me face first into the asphalt and I can't arrive at this meeting with a busted face."

My meeting with the execs at Theo's company was in the morning and I did a good job of pushing it out of my mind up until now so I could focus. I was so nervous in the weeks leading up to this moment, that I could barely function inside of my own body. My dad was worried I'd stumble my way into some stomach ulcers and my mom was worried I'd get so freaked out, that I'd turn down the opportunity all together.

Little did they know, there was no way in hell I was missing this chance to turn my life around and be the Ariana I was destined to be. Stomach ulcers or not, I was going to get on that plane and make this job my bitch. I managed to do the first part, now it was time to accomplish the second.

Nothing was going to get in my way.

Two

It's been two weeks since I first landed in Tokyo, and about a week since I started my new job as an intern research analyst.

When I went in to talk with the company executives to have an introductory meeting that told me what the company was about and what this job entailed, the end goal was just to set up a day and time for an interview. Fortunately for me, the executives liked me so much, they offered me the job right there on the spot, which thus began my journey with my new place of business, *FLEa Tech,* or, *Frontal Lobe Examination and Technology.*

Theo worked in another department that was located a few floors up from me, so we barely got a chance to see each other at work. My department worked in the basement of the building because that was the only logical place to keep all the big examination machines and rooms.

The company also provided me with living accommodations since I am moving from a whole new country and placed me in the apartment across the hall from Theodore's. Occasionally, we'll eat dinner together If he isn't working late, but he seems to always be working late these days.

Speaking of which, it was a Friday night and I happened to get off work a little bit earlier than usual. I usually leave the building when it's already dark outside, but this time, I managed to leave a little bit before the start of the sunset.

I text Theo earlier to see if he was working late again, and lo and behold, he was. I had nothing but time, which is something I barely had since my first night in Japan. I haven't even gotten a chance to really explore the city and to see what it had to offer me.

Since I'm alone and bored, with no food in my fridge, I figure it's as good a time as any to start my own personal Tokyo tour. Sure, I could wait until Theo was free, but I wanted to discover Japan through my own eyes and come up with my own favorites and conclusions rather than have premeditated opinions on things.

I grab my keys and purse off the kitchen counter, and head out into the Tokyo streets.

The first thing I decide to tackle is my irrefutable hunger because it'll only grow worse with each passing second. I decide to make a stop at the restaurant Theo took me to on my first night here because they really do have some good ass food.

After I fill my belly, I decide to just go with the flow of traffic and see where my feet take me. Tokyo reminded me so much of New York, with the high-intensity and colorful buildings and billboards. Also, the aggressiveness of the crowds and the times-squarey feeling I get when I walk down the street, as if I'm going to spot a set of stairs leading down to the subway everywhere I turn. It really was beautiful here, but the New York-esque of it all made me miss home terribly and made me miss my family even more.

I walk for about 15 minutes until a little pub to the right of me catches my eye. Well, technically the tree that was planted in a dumpster outside the pub caught my eye, but it made me curious as to what was in the actual building.

I was a nerd for hole-in-the-wall places that nobody really wants to give a chance, but once you do, it's the best place you've ever been to in your life.

I guess you can say that I'm attracted to the underrated and the overlooked. There was always beauty in them despite what the surface might show.

The bar I found was called Hatos Outside, and the inside didn't seem like it was meant to fit more than 20 people. There were about four small square tables against the far-left wall, and to the right was a little bar counter with a few barstools. The exposed ceiling was a charcoal gray with low hanging lightbulbs as chandeliers.

There were about 10 other people in here, taking up all the seats at the tables so I decide to sit at the bar.

I order a few drinks and laugh with the bartender and a few tourists who say they travel to Japan every year and never get tired of it.

By the time I step out of the pub, the sun had just set. It was almost 7:00 pm and I felt myself getting sleepy, because I'm usually settled into bed at this time. Still getting used to my 5:00 am work schedule.

I decided I've seen enough of Tokyo for tonight and would resume my tour sometime this weekend if I ever find the time. The alcohol was starting to work its way into my blood stream, but luckily, I didn't drink too much to where I couldn't walk straight.

I pass by a flower market that's starting to close its doors to breathe in the smell of the fresh white roses on a huge display outside the shop. Roses also reminded me of home because my mom had a garden window ledge she would teach me how to take care of as a kid. She always grew roses every spring and would cut them into a bouquet and give them to me for my birthday in August.

As I'm leaning down smelling the roses, out the corner of my eye, I see someone running at full speed out of an alleyway to the left of the flower market. He looks over his shoulder as if he's running away from someone and when he gets closer to me, his pace slows down a little.

He runs past me, and I turn my head to see where he's headed, but I'm caught by surprise when I see him kneeling behind the hedge of roses. He looks as though he's hiding from someone, and everything in me tells me to get the hell out of dodge, but a bigger piece of me says I should help this mysterious man.

I turn my body to where it's blocking any view of him from the side of the street he came running from. Just as I do this, I hear a loud commotion and what sounds like a stampede of animals coming from the alleyway he ran out of.

It was a group of women of all ages, ranging from what looked like teens to old grandmas. They were running in a crowd, bounding straight for me. They looked as though they just came from a concert, waving sharpies and posters in their hands, while all sporting the same looking t-shirts.

Most of them ran past me, but a couple of them eyed me wearily and decided to stop. They looked like a group of American tourists with their huge DSLR cameras hanging from their necks and their jackets tied around their waists.

"Have you seen Hendi? He ran this way, but we lost him."

Hendi?

"I'm sorry who?"

She looks at me with shock which quickly turns into disappointment before ultimately settling on disgust. She lets out a loud huff and stomps her feet as she tries to catch up to the crowd that was now a good 30 feet away.

The other girls give me the same disgusted look before following in her footsteps.

I watch them all leave and shake my head, turning it back towards the man I was covering, remembering that he was still there.

I take a step back, and he stands up from where he was kneeling, brushing off the soil from his knees that was left on the ground from the flower markets activities throughout the day.

When he finally looks back up, my breath hitches in my throat and forgets that it needs to go in and out of my body for me to survive. I swear the beauty on this man caused my brain to forget how to function, and that's never happened to me before.

He was about 6'2, wearing dark red plaid pants with so many zippers and chains on them that you'd think he was afraid he'd get pocket checked or something. His black V-neck t-shirt was figure hugging, so it showed off the muscle definition in his biceps as well as his abs. He was a slim guy but had muscles that made him look like he could hold me up with one hand while doing curl-ups with the other. His hair was jet black and looked unruly, I'm guessing from all the running he had to do to get away from the bevy of beauties screaming for him down the street.

He had a cigarette tucked behind his ear, and a vast array of rings decorating all of the fingers on both of his hands. His nails had patterns painted on them, one in particular being a skull head on his middle fingernail. He wore old, beat up looking Vans with the words "Not" written on the right shoe, and "Myself" written on the left in huge letters on the sides. He had a choker chain around his neck that matched the chains on his pants.

Once my brain kicks back into high gear, I realize we're both just standing here awkwardly, well more so awkward for him because I'm just ogling him the same way I'm sure those girls do.

Say something Ariana.

"Either you just did a really successful dine and dash, or your many wives just figured out they weren't the only apples of your eyes, let alone in your fruit basket." I joke and inwardly kick myself for accusing him of being a thief and an adulterer in one breath.

He lets out a chuckle that sounds like it came from deep within his chest, and the sound makes my stomach flip.

"Thanks for letting me hide in your roses," he says, and his deep gravelly voice just sends my senses into an even bigger frenzy.

I look at him confused, and realize he probably thinks I work at this flower shop. I put my hands up and wave them furiously, struggling to find my words again.

"Oh no no, I don't work here. I'm just visiting," I say quickly, surprised I made a coherent sentence.

He lifts up an eyebrow and simultaneously nodding his head like he understands me completely before saying, "Ah, so you're a tourist then."

His accent sounds oddly American, so I assume he's not from around here either.

"Not necessarily. I've been living here the past couple of weeks, so I'd like to consider myself an official resident."

I don't know why I'm telling this man my business, he can be a serial killer for all I know. Just because he had a group of girls chasing after him didn't mean he wasn't dangerous. Girls these days have the hots for dangerously toxic men who have, in fact, murdered a few people, thanks to Netflix's depiction of their lives.

Somehow despite all of the warning signs and red flags that should be going up right about now, I feel oddly calm and comfortable with this gorgeous stranger.

"Give it a few months before calling yourself a resident. There's no way you've seen all of Japan that fast." He retorts to me, while pulling his phone out of his back pocket and scrolling through what looked like endless notifications.

"And let me guess, you know all there is to know about Japan because you've been living here for many *many* years," I say doing air quotes as I emphasize my last few words.

"No, I just happen to be here a lot, so I know all of the best places for anything you're looking for."

I scoff at him, and that makes him smile, causing his diamond stud nose ring to shimmer in the night light.

Oh God, that smile will be the end of me.

"*Anything* I'm looking for? What if I wanted to find an all-nude bar that served drinks on the back of a goat?"

He laughs and I pat myself on the back for being possessed with the ability to make gorgeous alphas almost drop to their knees in laughter.

"Weird, but I can take you somewhere that caters to all of your needs." He says still laughing.

He looks down at the watch he was sporting on his left wrist, then squints his eyes towards me as if he's conjuring up a plan.

"What are your plans for the rest of the night?" He finally asks and the question catches me all the way off guard.

"Plans? I don't really—"

"Good. I'm going to take you on your own personal tour of Tokyo." He states as if he's just set it in stone.

He grabs my wrist, and his touch sends a jolt of electricity up my arm and through the rest of my body. I follow behind him for a second before my brain takes control again and causes me to stop walking.

When he realized I wasn't going to move anymore, he looked back at me with confusion in his gaze.

"Wait a minute," I start to say as I reluctantly pull my wrist free from his hold. "I just met you not even 10 minutes ago, and you expect me to go somewhere with you in a foreign place I'm just now getting the hang of? How do I know you aren't a murderer or a sex trafficker trying to lure me into the jaws of death? You never even told me your name, nor did you ask me for mine."

He runs a hand through his hair and lets out a deep breath. "You're right, I'm sorry. I just get a little too excited when it comes to doing spontaneous things."

He stops talking and turns to look at me, eyeing me suspiciously.

"You really don't know who I am?"

I scrunch my eyebrows together, confused as hell. Am I supposed to know who this man is?

I cross my arms and wait for him to explain further because I'm about 2 milliseconds away from walking back in the other direction towards my apartment. I'm surprised Theo hasn't sent his "You awake" text yet seeing as it was after 8:00 pm. He usually would text me as soon as he got in to see if I wanted to grab a bite to eat or something.

The guy in front of me shakes his head disbelievingly before continuing. "Hendi," he says as he extends out his hand to me, "And you are?"

"Ariana," I say, shaking his hand back, ignoring the hyperawareness of the shockwave pulsating through my body. "Is Hendi your full name?"

"No, it's short for Hendrix, but people just call me Hendi."

I realize I'm still holding his hand long after the shake was finished, and pull away, hiding the redness I feel staining my cheeks.

"Now that that's out the way, you ready to get the best night of your life started?" He asks me with a huge boyish grin displayed across his very manly, very comfortable looking face.

"I never agreed to go anywhere with you. Just because I know your name doesn't make you any less of a serial killer." I say defiantly.

He scratches his chin, probably trying to figure out an excuse to get me to follow him anywhere, even if into a sketchy looking white van.

"What if I let you hold on to my wallet and personal belongings?"

"Still means nothing if you smack me across the head and throw me in a trunk."

"You drive a hard bargain Ms.Ariana." He looks as though he's still not going to give up until a lightbulb almost seems to visibly appear over his head by the way his face lit up.

He held up one finger towards me as if telling me to wait one moment, and fished his phone back out of his back pocket. He did a lot of navigating and scrolling before he landed on what he was searching for.

He held out his phone to me, and I took it so I could examine what it was he was showing me. On the phone was a picture of Hendi sharing a friendly bro handshake-hug with someone. This someone was not just any someone though, this someone was *the* Barack Obama, former president of the United States.

My mouth goes slack and Hendi grabs the phone back, a satisfied smirk on his face as he tucks it back into his pocket.

"Would I be friends with the president If I was a serial killer?" He ends his argument with that final question.

Plenty of serial killers were seen shaking hands with the presidents, but since it was Barack, I decide to let him have his way. Besides, I'm curious to know how a 23-year-old looking man managed to become friends with *the* Barack Obama.

"Fine, you win. But I need the back story." I say to him as he fist pumps his hand in the air in triumph.

"I'll tell you while we head to our first destination little grasshopper."

"Grasshopper? What is this the Karate Kid?"

Three

I tried to take a guess at where Hendi was taking me the whole way to the first destination, but boy was I way off. I never would've guessed where we actually ended up going.

"Which hat screams 'I'm a regular citizen just like you, please keep your claws and handcuffs away'?" Hendi asks from the other side of the clothing rack.

We were at what looked like a bodega but for clothes so Hendi could pick out a disguise. There was a vast array of clothes on racks outside as well as inside the store. He said it was crucial he had a disguise so this private tour can go smoothly without groups of screaming girls coming after him.

I need to figure out who exactly this man is that I decided to spend a couple of hours with on a random Friday night. I could google him, but where's the fun in that?

"Handcuffs?" I quirk an eyebrow at him over the clothing rack.

He adjusts the baseball cap he placed carefully on his head to where it was covering most of his forehead, then turned from the mirror he was bending down to peak into. He places dark Ray Bans over his beautiful light brown eyes, hiding them from the world.

"You'd be surprised at the shit I've seen and been through," he says, pulling his wallet out one of the many zippers in his pants.

We walk up to the counter and he takes out a few bills from his wallet. He then looks at me, and even though I could barely see his face, his gaze made me feel slightly naked and exposed.

"You want a disguise too? It's fun pretending to be someone you're not. We could even create our own story."

"Oh, you mean like you could be my mother's boy toy who ended up falling in love with me, but you got my mom pregnant instead?"

"You have an interesting weird mind, you know that?" he says as he taps my left temple. "I was thinking more along the lines of, we could be a newly married couple on our honeymoon, seeing the world one train stop at a time."

"How romantic," I fake swoon and head back towards the rack of clothes. It does sound fun to be someone else, and besides, it's only for a night. What harm would that do?

"You sure your girlfriend won't mind you entertaining another woman for a night?" I graze my fingertips along the clothes on the rack in front of me.

"I'm sure she would if I had one. I don't do monogamy. It gets too messy, and besides, I'm always travelling so it'll never work."

I peer up at him over the rack, "Too good for long distance?"

He hikes one shoulder up. "It's not that, I just don't have the time, energy, or mental capacity for something like that."

"That makes sense," I say mostly to myself and leave the subject alone, even though I have more questions.

I settle on a black bodycon dress, with a baseball cap that matched Hendi's. I went into the dressing room to change, and when I emerged, I heard him whistle from the wall he was leaning against.

"You look hot Mrs. Hendi."

"Ha ha. Where do I put my clothes?" I ask, looking around to see if the store sold any bags.

"Just leave them in the dressing room and come on. We have lots to see and too little time to see them." He grabs the clothes from my hand and tosses them into the dressing room.

Grabbing my wrist, he leads me past the cashier and out to the busy Tokyo streets.

"Wait! We didn't pay!" I say trying to pull out of his grasp.

"Don't worry about that, just worry about the amount of fun you're about to have." He pulls out his phone and types something before turning placing it back in his bag.

"Now I know having dessert before dinner spoils your appetite, but I couldn't deprive your sweet little taste buds from this goodness any longer. We'll just push the actual food stop to later in the tour."

After a few minutes of speed walking (basically running) here, we made it outside of a nice yellow brick looking building titled *Tomihisa*. It was sitting between what appeared to be a crab shack and a woman's wax center or something.

I look down next to my feet and take in the small ice cream cone sculpture sitting out front of the ice cream shop that looked like it's been closed for hours now.

"Um, I hate to burst your bubble but...I think they're closed." I say pointing my finger towards the shop.

He shakes his head at me then walks up to the shop door. "I didn't peg you as one to see the glass half empty. Watch and learn grasshopper."

He pulls out a bobby pin from his pocket and proceeds to literally pick the lock.

I walk up to him and punch his strong, tennis ball looking bicep.

"Hendi!" I whisper shout, "That's breaking and entering! What if we get caught?"

I turn back around, looking from side to side at the street and the people walking by, casually waving and giving an awkward smile, while yet again, trying to shield what Hendi is doing from view.

How many times am I going to have to hide this man tonight?

"Hendrix!" I whisper shout again, turning completely to him once the ghost was clear. He stopped picking for a moment before resuming.

Not even 30 seconds later, the door clicks open and he gives me a broad grin. I shake my head at him, and he pushes the shop door open. A loud siren blares through the shop and pierces my ears, causing me to almost shit myself.

He saunters over to the alarm system as if it wasn't stabbing his eardrums over and over like mine, and types in a code, causing the sound to quiet immediately.

Does he own this shop? How many layers does this man have?

Now that my anxiety and fear of being arrested for breaking and entering is calming down (not fully though), I take in the aesthetic of the ice cream shop.

There was a huge white and blue countertop taking up majority of the space in this cute little shop. The cooler where the ice cream is held is empty and I'm assuming the actual ice cream is stored in the back freezer for the next time they open.

There were signs everywhere advertising the price and different pastries offered. Once I finish my eye tour, I settle my gaze on Hendrix who's just watching me behind his dark Ray Bans.

Either that or he fell asleep leaning on the counter.

"You like?" he finally asks, pushing off the counter.

I nod my head slowly as he lifts the counter he was leaning on, and gestures for me to walk through.

"After you," he bows, and I can't help the girlish giggle that slips past my mouth.

Normally, all the flags that have been thrown at my face would cause me to see nothing but red, but Hendi makes me feel oddly comfortable.

It's actually *uncomfortable* how comfortable I feel around him.

I walk to the back of the ice cream shop and the draft in the kitchen instantly causes goosebumps to form all over my arms. I shudder involuntarily and rub them to keep warm. The feel of Hendi's warm chest against my back and his arms encompassing me from behind cause me to jump away.

"I'm sorry you just looked—" he starts.

"It's okay, you just caught me by surprise, that's all," I cut him off quickly to avoid an awkward moment.

I look around at all the silver appliances and coolers that decorate this backroom before taking a seat at the small round wooden table in the left corner. Hendi walks over to the cooler that seems to hold all the ice cream flavors and grabs a scooper from the drawer next to it.

He starts to scoop a blue colored glop of ice cream and places it carefully in a waffle bowl. He adds a pink colored one, and then a lime green one. He reaches to his left with practiced ease, drizzling a red syrup over the top as if he's sprinkling parsley on top, finishing off his masterpiece.

He turns to me with a sinister smile, and glides across the room exuding confidence and self-assurance.

He places the concoction on the table in front of him and sits down, licking his lips. He raises his right hand, revealing a spoon he must've grabbed on his journey to the table.

One spoon.

One.

He places the spoon in the ice cream, and slowly gathers a portion that contains every ingredient he added to the waffle bowl.

He raises the spoon towards his mouth, and my eyes dart to the bob of his Adams apple and the veins lining his neck. My eyes move back to the spoon that's just chilling in mid-air and then to his eyes that show he's having fun teasing me with this ice cream.

"I'm sorry, did you want some?" he cocks his eyebrow up and struggles to keep his face straight.

"I thought you said you couldn't 'deprive my sweet little taste buds'?"

"I did say that, didn't I?" He moves the spoon across the table and I instinctively open my mouth to welcome what I hope is a heavenly mixture of sweets.

As he feeds me this spoonful of ice cream, the bottom of the spoon brushes the bottom of my lip, causing a trickle of ice cream to slide down the side of my mouth.

I'm too busy enjoying and having a mouth-gasm at what tastes like cold cotton candy mixed with tropical fruits form some foreign island, to realize what Hendi is doing before it's too late.

He reaches across the table, brushing his thumb across the ice cream stream, then brings said thumb to his mouth, sucking on it.

My mouth almost falls open, but thankfully a small part of my brain wasn't fried from how hot that was.

His eyes never left mine during that whole exchange, and my face grows hot from how naked I feel right now under his lustful gaze. Desperate for a change of pace before things get carried away too fast, I clear my throat and grab the bowl of ice cream that's still sitting in front of him and stab my spoon into it, collecting a huge chunk.

"So, Hendi, tell me…are you some famous ice cream chef trying to steal the taste buds of all the beautiful women across the world?" I fix my eyes on the chunk I'm holding in front of my mouth, too nervous to look him in the eyes again.

He releases a low chuckle and I feel him shaking his head no.

"I'm actually really good friends with the owner. He owes me a few favors too, and I decided to cash out on one of them early."

He reaches across the table and grabs the ice cream as I put the spoon back in. He grabs himself a chunk and puts it in his mouth.

This guy obviously wasn't a germophobe, or even cared about germs at all.

He didn't seem opposed to questions, so I decided now was a better time than any to find out what I wanted to know.

"How did you know you could trust me?" I ask genuinely curious.

He stops moving the ice cream carefully around in his mouth and looks at me confused.

"What do you mean?"

"I mean, you're obviously a guy who is well known around here, so how'd you know you could trust me not to be like those girls that were chasing you down earlier?"

It takes him no time at all to say his answer.

"Because you looked at me as if I was a psycho." He grabs another scoop and places it in his mouth, then slides the bowl across the table back to me.

Now I'm the one sporting a confused face while he sits there looking as if his answer makes perfect sense.

"What?" I say laughing a little.

He hitches one shoulder up and rests his arm on the back of the chair he's sitting in, getting more comfortable.

"You looked at me like I was a crazy person leading a riot down the street. You looked like you wanted nothing to do with my mess which made me want to bring my mess to you even more. I was intrigued to say the least."

I shake my head at him and absent mindedly scoop ice cream into my mouth. His slow smile reminds me that we're sharing saliva and all types of viruses. Surprisingly, I'm not as disgusted or turned off as I thought I'd be.

This interaction was more intimate than I'd ever been with my one and only ex-boyfriend.

"You're right. I wanted nothing to do with what you were dragging behind you." I say playfully, but true.

"So, you do want something to do with *me?*" He challenges and I feel my face getting warm again. He shakes his head before I open my mouth. "Forget that question. What made you trust me?"

He throws my question right back at me and I smile.

"Your craziness. Something inside me said you were a good crazy and that I should accept what you were offering. Just for one night," I look down and realize I ate all of the ice cream and feel a slight amount of disappointment at the fact I won't have anymore.

He stands up causing me to jerk my attention back to his face, and he has an easy smile on. He holds his hand out to me then shows off his teeth.

"Your adventure awaits."

I smile back up at him and grab his hand.

Somehow, I feel like I'm offering him more than just my hand.

Four

"When you want to get away and channel your inner kid spirit, this is the perfect place to go," Hendrix says as he expands his arms out wide towards the huge building in front of us that reads Joypolis.

We walk through the glass front doors and the first thing that comes to my mind when I see the lobby is "futuristic". I take in all the silver space station looking directions and the people all talking and laughing with their kids or groups of friends.

In the middle, there's a circular post that looks like a directory. The tv screens showed what looked like cues, but I couldn't understand any of it because it was all in Japanese.

Hendi places his hand on my lower back and guides me forward towards the section that says

Joypolis Sega and is blocked off by modernized looking subway gates. There was a circular glass door with the initials "JP" on them, below an entrance sign.

"You first grasshopper," he says as he scans a card he produced from his pocket onto the scanner, causing the doors to open, letting me through. He does the same for himself so we're both on the same side of the gates and walk through the entrance.

How was he able to get prepared this fast for my "private tour"? Was this something he did with one lucky girl every night?

I turn my head to look up at him and find him already watching me.

"Is this okay?" he gestures towards the arcade looking amusement park.

I nod excitedly as I look around and take in all the rides and attractions, feeling my inner kid-self buzzing with excitement.

"This is perfect, but how did you already have one of those cards?"

He shrugs nonchalantly, "I love it here, so I always keep my membership card on me."

I nod accepting his answer and think about which attraction I want to try first.

"You sure this is okay? I mean I can take you somewhere else—"

"Hendi, this is fine. I promise."

As we walk over to the information desk, he shakes his head, a small smile on his face.

"What?" I ask him, bumping my shoulder into his arm.

"Nothing," he replies and turns his head to the man behind the desk. He speaks fluent Japanese to him, catching me all the way off guard.

He gestures towards me and the guy behind the desk laughs before scanning a member card and handing it to me. I grab it, giving a polite smile even though I'm almost sure they're making fun of me.

"Arigatōgozaimashita," Hendi bows towards the man and places his hand back on the spot on my lower back.

"You're fluent in Japanese? Is there anything you can't do?" I ask in disbelief.

He lets out a loud laugh, throwing his head back, giving me a great look at his beautiful profile.

"There's a lot I can't do L.G., but I'm always in Japan for work so it makes sense for me to learn the language. Besides, I consider Tokyo my second home and I respect and love the culture here."

Always in Japan for work?

L.G.?

Before I have a chance to ask him more questions, he grabs my hand and lightly pulls me towards the escalators.

"Shouldn't we start on the first floor?" I nod my head towards the claw machines to the left.

"I'm not one to follow the rules L.G.," he winks down at me and my insides melt, forgetting what it was I was talking about.

We get off the escalators and he leads me over to these space ship looking cars on a raised platform.

"Up for a little friendly competition?" he challenges me as we take our place in line.

"You obviously don't know who I am. I remain undefeated at *all* of Dave & Buster's car racing games." I crack my knuckles, then neck, as I roll my shoulders and bounce from foot to foot like Rocky.

He laughs that gorgeous, panty melting laugh again, this time letting his shoulders join in and places his hand over his chest.

"You look crazy right now. Besides, you're right, I don't know you, but that'll change by the end of the night."

There's an underlying message to his statement that makes the already alive butterflies in my stomach become hyperactive as if they're on a sugar high.

After what feels like 20 races because he couldn't accept the fact he was losing, I pulled a sulking Hendi away from the space cars and we went over to the indoor roller coaster.

"Just so you know, I'm deathly terrified of roller coasters," I say next to him in line. We progress forward and I can feel my anxiety climbing up my throat, desperate for air.

He grabs my hand and gives me a reassuring squeeze and I take this opportunity to "accidentally" brush my thumb across his knuckles. You know, just trying to get a feel of his skin to see if it's as soft as it looks.

It was way softer than I could ever imagine. Like rubbing my hand across velvet. This man must exfoliate his skin twice a day or something.

I don't realize it's our turn in line until I feel Hendi giving me a light tug.

"You okay?" he asks, concern etched in his features.

In my mind, my head shakes violently, protesting this devil contraption and whoever built it. In my mind, I'm kicking and screaming saying I don't want to do this and that I'd rather eat a million fire ants before stepping my feet into one of those four seats.

My body betrays my mind though because I feel myself nodding yes.

"It'll be okay. This is just a coaster, so it isn't as intense as the real thing. Plus, I'm right here, although, it's only 95% of me seeing as you crushed the other 5% to death."

I look down at our hands and see that I am indeed, squeezing his for dear life and let it go.

"Sorry," I say quietly as the worker impatiently ushers me into the front two seats.

Hendi climbs in next to me, and we get our handlebars fastened on top of us. He leans over and whispers in my ear.

"I want you to let go of that fear and enjoy this moment."

With those words, I do just that. Like magic, the anxiety melts out of me, seeping through my pores and onto the ground in front of me. I let in a long breath and release it on a freeing exhale. He squeezes my knee, putting the last nail on the confidence coffin (And pulling out a nail from my metaphorical chastity belt).

The ride begins to move, but his hand remains rested on my knee. I squeeze my eyes shut, but he squeezes my knee again causing them to open.

"Uh uh," he wags his finger when I look at him, "Enjoy the moment."

"So… you're afraid of roller coasters? Why?" He asks, taking a bite of the caramel vanilla cookie crepe he insisted I try at the crepe shop in here. This man has a serious sweet tooth.

"You eat a lot of sweets. Why?" I grab the crepe from his hand as he goes to get another bite. I take a piece with my fork and let the fluffy, chewy dough caress my taste buds.

"You ask a lot of questions," he flicks my ear softly and my face grows red from the heat that rushes to my cheeks. I'm pretty sure I broke the world record of how many times a person can blush in one night.

"You started it. I'm not one to willingly give information without getting it in return," I scoop the last bite the crepe off the plate and start bringing it up to my face. Hendi grabs my wrist and moves it to where the fork is facing him, bends down, and slowly takes the piece off while staring at me in the face. I felt his gaze through his sunglasses.

Looks like I should've bought an extra pair of panties from the clothing shop earlier.

A smirk hit his face and I knew then that he was teasing me. Trying to get a reaction. This must be what he does with all of his other girls.

He stands up straight and gestures toward a bench with race car looking wheels on each side. I take a seat and he plops down next to me, leaning back and draping his arm along the back of the bench, so close to touching my shoulder that it almost tickles.

"Well, growing up, I had to watch my little brother, Ozzy, a lot. I was only 8 and he was 4, but I was responsible for dinner 95% of the time. I didn't know how to cook an actual meal and I just reached the height to where I could cook ramen noodles on the stove by myself. Well, one night, we didn't have ramen noodles or anything else for a main course, so I had to improvise."

"Let me guess, ice cream for dinner?" I ask, amused and interested to learn more about his story. Why was he responsible for him and his brother? Where were his parents?

"Yep, a whole bunch of it. Of course, we loved it because we were kids. What kid doesn't want ice cream for dinner every night?" He's smiling but his smile is sad as he recalls the memory. Something in me wants to take away all the bad him and his brother endured and hug him while telling him it's okay.

"I'm pretty sure the lactose intolerant kids don't," I offer jokingly.

He actually laughs and I inwardly fist pump at this small feat.

"Even lactose intolerant kids will eat that shit up. They think it's worth all the pain, which is true." He trails off, lost in what looks like a bad memory before remembering where he is.

"Anyway, to answer your question, sweets have always been a comfort food for me because it reminded me of all the fun Ozzy and I had as kids, despite our *situation*. So, every time I eat sweets, I think of him."

Situation?

"Aw, that's so sweet. No pun intended. You guys must be really close then?" I look down at my legs, kicking my feet like a little schoolgirl or something. I was just trying to find something to do with myself to keep from making him feel awkward.

"I'll do anything for him," he says more seriously. "What about you though? Any siblings? Whether estranged, stupid, or unbearable?"

I throw my head back and laugh, shaking my head. "I wish. My parents never gave me that luxury of having a forever best friend. I've always wanted one though and practically begged them every day until I was in middle school."

"Well, you're definitely missing out LG."

I look around at the attractions we have yet to try, then hop up from my seat. I turn back, looking down at him and quirk my eyebrow.

"I'm taking control of this tour for a second and demanding you to take me on more cool rides."

"Wait but you haven't even answered my first que—"

"You're wasting too much time talking and not enough time 'funning'."

"Funning?" He stands up from his seat, an easy smile replacing the sad one.

"Yep, our new word only valid for the remainder of the night."

I turn to start walking towards the line of treadmills that look like they could be a racing game. Hendi grabs my elbow softly and turns me around to face him. He's very handsy and very controlling it seems. Some might see this as a red flag, but I see it differently. I don't know much about his past, only the information he just gave, but it doesn't take a rocket scientist to put two and two together. I think him having to raise his little brother caused him to become protective and take the lead in a lot of situations.

He leans down, brushing his lips against my ear. "I will get the answers to all of my questions before the night is over *Ariana.*"

He drags out my name in a slow seductive taunt, causing the hair all over my body to shoot up in attention. A shiver slides across my body and he releases my elbow, causing me to sway slightly before regaining my footing.

This was going to be a long night.

We rode literally every ride in there, even the roller coaster again a couple more times before calling it quits for this stop. My stomach started to cry out for real food and not the sweets Hendi has been trying to fill me up on.

"Someone's hungry," he chuckles down towards me.

"I mean, you have been dragging me all around the world without any *real* food." I say a tiny bit snappier than I meant to say because I am hungry.

"Not all around the world, just Tokyo. Maybe if you're good, you'll get to see the world." He raises his sunglasses for a brief moment to wink at me, then sets them back in their comfortable spot on his face. A spot I wish I could comfortably be.

What the hell am I thinking? The hunger is getting to me.

I roll my eyes toward him as he walks off, leaving me behind. Letting out a huff, I follow behind him like a lost puppy, hoping he's taking me to get food now.

Five

After walking about 30 minutes, Hendi decided he let me suffer enough, and we got on a train at the Shijō-mae station.

The trains in Tokyo were worlds away from the trains in New Jersey. They had actual cushions on them to make the ride somewhat comfortable. It didn't even have that mildew smell from stale pee mixed with whatever gunk was plastered all over the subway floors in Jersey. The station here was surprisingly clean.

I could get used to the Tokyo lifestyle.

There's only one spot available in the car we walked on, so Hendi told me to sit and he stood protectively to the side of me. I lean back into the cushion and take this time to examine him a little closer. He has rings dressed on all his fingers except the middle on his left hand. A small detail I didn't notice when I first sized him up. He has a red electric guitar tattooed along the side of his forearm and the words "au clair de la lune" outlining the side of his palm just below the bottom of the guitar.

He also has vines and cherry blossom flowers entangling the guitar, making it seem like his body was a tree and the roots captured the guitar, trying to draw it in and absorb it into the main trunk.

He was beyond gorgeous and I'm suddenly jealous of all the girls he's probably gone to bed with in the past. I know I don't have the right to be jealous, but I can't help it. The man is like a living sculpture meant to be on display in The Louvre.

A couple stops later, a spot next to me clears and Hendi hurriedly sits down before the guy that's been eyeing me across the car, got the chance. When he sees that Hendi is possibly the man in my life, he retreats deeper into the car and I let out a small giggle.

He glances at me and offers a boyish smile, "That's a cute noise. You should let it out more often."

I suppress the blush that wants to break free.

"So. Roller coasters. Talk." He props his right ankle on his left knee and holds onto it with both hands, peering at me over the top of his glasses. His hat is lifted a little, so his forehead is exposed, and his hat hair is peeking through.

"You won't give up, will you? It's not even that crazy of a reason." I shake my head knowing he'll be disappointed once I finally spill the information I'd been withholding.

"I still want to know," he says simply. I breathe out in defeat.

"I just hate the tickly feeling I get in my stomach from the drops. That's all."

His eyes widen like I grew two heads, then drops his head between his shoulders briefly before looking back at me.

"You do realize that's the best part, right?" He cocks his eyebrow up and I shrug nonchalantly.

"To *you.*"

"To *everyone.*"

"What are you? The spokesperson for the world?" I tap my forefinger on my chin, "That must be why you had those girls chasing you."

"Something like that," he gives that devilish smile again and I know that I'm in danger.

The train comes to a stop and the conductor says something in Japanese over the intercom.

"Saved by the bell," Hendi says while listening to the announcement, "We're the next stop."

We enter the elevator of a building that holds multiple shops, just like most of the places around Japan. Hendi wouldn't let me look at the titles of the places in this building so I would be caught by surprise.

He pushes the button for floor 7, and the elevator starts to move. Above the elevator buttons, there's a welcome sign with a dancing skeleton and smiling pumpkin. I look at Hendi with a raised brow, questioning the fact that he might be a serial killer again.

We step off the elevator, and the first thing I notice is the bright red floor, decorated with blood cells all over. A voice stops me from staring at the floor, and I see there's a man standing a few feet in front of us.

He's dressed from head to toe in vampire looking clothing, including the face make-up, fangs, and black colored fingernails. I realize the voice that I heard was Hendi's, telling the man something in Japanese, and the vampire gestures for us to follow him.

As the guy leads us down this hallway draped in red curtains and the floor still decorated with blood cells, I whisper to Hendi, "what the hell?"

He ignores me and places his muscular hand on the lower part of my back that causes heat to erupt all over my body.

The vampire leads us into a room and stops us on the threshold before saying something else in Japanese. Female waitresses respond to him in unison before looking at us and smiling.

There's a real-life coffin on the floor in front of me draped with flowers and candles, tucked under a round table with chairs to the right. On the stone wall directly to my right, there's a gold floor to ceiling mirror next to a cabinet with different clutter items placed all over it.

Beside the round table over the coffin, there are two other black tables with gold trim in the middle of the room, oval in shape and could fit four people on each. The chairs are a smooth red color and also trimmed in gold.

Along the walls are private booths, separated by the same red curtains. The vampire leads us directly to the wall straight ahead to a private booth. I take a step up onto the platform before taking a seat in the black cushioned booth. Hendi climbs in after me, and I move to where we're facing each other without straining.

The restaurant isn't packed, but it has , a good amount of people inside. A waitress wearing a black maid outfit brings us menus and Hendi tells her something before she leaves.

I make a mental note to sign up to learn Japanese while I'm here.

I take in all the décor and the ambiance of the building, genuinely impressed with how well it was put together.

"Ready to eat?" Hendi asks, looking relaxed in his seat across from me.

"Of course, but I don't know what I want. This place is …different."

"You want to go somewhere else?" he sits up, looking ready to get up whenever I say the word.

"No, I want to experience everything you're trying to show me. Besides, I'm sure you chose this place for a reason." I show him that I'm okay with this by picking up the menu then my phone so I can pull up the English version online like the menu prompts at the top.

"You'll see," he says, not looking at his menu.

A second later, the waitress brings us a plate with four little cross shaped breads topped with a dollop of something I can't recognize.

"What is that?" I ask him when she walks away again.

"Taste it," he orders me, ignoring my question.

I do as I'm told and place a cross in my mouth, closing my eyes as the taste hits my tongue. So different from anything I've ever tasted. So filled with flavor, it should be illegal.

"Oh my god," I moan, "That's so good."

"I know," he says, a cocky tone lacing his voice. He takes off his shades and hooks them on his V-neck. My eyes grow wide and I look around quickly before leaning in.

"Are you sure that's a good idea? What if people recognize you?" I whisper. Even though I don't know what he does or who exactly he is, I *am* smart enough to know he must be a public figure who is extremely famous or maybe almost extremely famous.

"Yea, it's safe here," he shrugs one of his shoulders, then grabs a cross cracker.

That's when it hits me.

"Is this your way of telling me you're secretly a vampire? And this whole night was just a plot to sweeten my blood up with activity and sugar so you can drain it out of my body later?"

I take in the eerie ambience of the vampire themed restaurant. There was a literal coffin in the room in front of a Victorian style, floor to ceiling mirror. The stoned walls and red draping curtains everywhere made me feel like I was an extra in a Vampire Diaries episode.

"What makes you think I'm a vampire?" he asks, almost choking on the cracker.

"Well, for starters, you and our vampire friend both have rings covering all of your fingers. You both have dark brooding features. You seem overly active at night, and it seems like you come here often."

He pretends to pull an imaginary cape over the lower half of his face before saying, "Ah, you've foiled my plan."

He laughs an evil laugh and I throw one of the cross-shaped crackers at him. He dodges it with such grace and it further confirms my theory of him being a mystical creature.

"I guess it's good I didn't take you to the hedgehog café. You probably would've thrown one of them at me." He laughs as he says this then picks up the cross and hurls it back at me. It lands next to me on the booth and I tuck it back on the plate where it came from.

"Did you just say hedgehog café? As in live, cute, pigmy hedgehogs?" I ask in disbelief.

"So, you've heard of them?" He grabs a cross and takes a bite.

"Heard of them? I used to watch videos of them getting a bath on YouTube when I was younger. You did good by taking me here instead though because I would've been playing with them the whole time and not eating."

He shakes his head at me, a smile pulling at his lips.

Six

For the next couple hours, we talk about everything and nothing while simultaneously filling our bellies with more vampire themed food. We discuss politics, our favorite colors, and other small things before the real questions start to pour in.

"What's your full name?" I ask sipping on my electric blue drink. We finished eating all our food an hour ago and just got lost in conversation. That caused me to gain enough courage to ask him more personal questions.

"Oh, down to the deeper questions I see." He jokes.

"It's just your name," I softly roll my eyes while smiling.

"My name holds a lot of weight LG. Anyway, it's Hendrix Evans. No middle name because my parents didn't think I needed one." His foot brushes my leg under the table, and I'm guessing it's to distract me into answering his personal questions. "How about you? What's your full name LG?"

"Ariana Marcelle McNally. I go by Ari though."

His face looks amused and he nods his head slowly in an "I hear you" gesture.

"You also go by LG." He points at me with the hand that's holding his own electric blue drink before taking a swig.

"Or I'm just tolerating it for tonight because even if I tell you not to, you'd keep calling me that."

He chuckles, "you know me so well already *Ariana*."

How could this man make any word sound like sex?

He makes me want to record him saying my name so I can set it as my ringtone.

"So LG, where are you from? And how did a girl like you end up in Tokyo?"

A girl like me?

"I'm from Newark, New Jersey, but unlike everyone else in my family, you wouldn't be able to tell just by looking at me." I lean back in the booth, rubbing my overly expanded belly in satisfaction.

"Jokes on you. I could tell you were from Jersey the moment I saw you." He repositions the hat on his head before draping his arm over the back of the booth, getting comfortable like me.

"Oh? How so?" I ask, curious and probably falling for a childish trap.

He leans forward and assesses my face before speaking again.

"You weren't afraid to speak your mind, even if it wasn't with your words. Also, you're funny. Case closed."

I shake my head at that horrible explanation.

"So… how does that mean I'm from Jersey?"

"Well, I've travelled to *a lot* of places and experienced a lot of different cultures. It's safe to say that people from New Jersey are the funniest people on earth. Also, you guys say whatever comes to your head without care."

I don't say anything to this because he's spot on. I thought he was going to say because I have an accent which would've been a lie because for some odd reason, I don't have that deep Jersey accent like the rest of my family. It's a crazy miracle that they've been trying to solve for years.

"Okay. What about you *Hendi*? Where are you from?" I lean forward, lacing my hands together and resting my chin on top of them.

"Born in Nashville but moved to this small city known as Manhattan when I was two. So, I guess we've been somewhat like neighbors for a few years." His eyes brighten at this realization that we've been close to each other but have never crossed paths.

"How old are you?" A question that's been at the back of my mind the whole time we've been together.

His face looks like he's around my age but his eyes--- those gorgeous beautiful eyes--- say that he's seen a lot of things and has endured a lot of pain. The type of pain that can cause you to either give into your demons or claw your way back to your angels.

"Just turned 24 a few months ago. Taurus."

That explains his goofiness and protective nature. He looks at me questioningly, waiting for me to disclose my age.

"I'm turning 22 in a couple of months. Scorpio." If he feels some type of way about this, he doesn't show it. He just rests his hand on his chin.

"Did you go to college?" His hand now mindlessly caressing his chin.

I nod my head, but don't disclose what school I went too. I raise my eyebrow at him, and he just shakes head.

"I never got the chance to go to college. It's always been something I wanted to experience though." Sadness flickers in his eyes for a moment before he covers it again with amusement.

"It's never too late for college," I give off an encouraging tone and he gives a small smile in return.

"It's too late to experience it how I wanted to experience it. Besides, I don't need college 'cause I already landed my *dream job*." He puts "dream job" in air quotes and that gesture alone sparks my curiosity even more.

"And what job is that?" I ask, watching his hand as it goes back and forth against his chin. I swallow hard.

"Too early in the night to disclose that information LG. Let's just leave some mystery so it can still be fun." He winks and closes the curtains to our booth, so we're completely disclosed in it.

He takes off his hat and runs his hands through his hair, knocking me out with his beauty.

"So you're an only child. If you could choose, would you have a little brother or sister?" He flashes a boyish smile when he realizes I'm staring at him. Leaning across the table, he uses his forefinger to close the mouth I didn't know was stuck open and brushes his finger lightly underneath my chin.

I stagger, unable to find my words, and if I was standing up, I would've lost my footing and my knees would've buckled.

"I-I always wanted a little brother." Now I'm stuttering. Just great. Get yourself together Ariana.

"Did you tell your parents that?" He chuckles and I know he's laughing at me and how stupid I must've looked just then. Heat rushes up my face and I sink down lower into my seat, trying to hide myself from this man's intense gaze.

"Yea, I used to beg them all the time. They kept using the excuse of me being enough for them and that I already had a brother in my childhood best friend. I was mad at them for a long time, but eventually got over it when I got to middle school."

"You should've found their condom stash and poked holes in all of them." He suggests.

I gasp in horror and he shrugs his shoulders while laughing.

"Is Ozzy your only sibling?"

"As far as I know," he quips. "What's your family like?"

I sit up straight and think about this question and how I want to answer. Based on what he said at Joypolis, I can already assume that he didn't have the best family life growing up.

"They're supportive…loving…and very hardworking. It's just me, my dad, and my mom now. Yea I have distant family, but I don't really know them like that."

He listens intently as I tell him about my dad owning his own business and my mom being the one to help put it all in motion. I don't mention my grandfather.

"It sounds like you have a great family. Don't ever take them for granted." His tone sounds serious and I do my best to not take offense to his statement.

I decide to shift gears because he obviously isn't ready to reveal too much about himself.

"So, are you going to tell me how you managed to break into that ice cream shop earlier?"

Amusement rolls of his body, replacing all his tension.

"I was wondering when you were going to ask about that." He doesn't say anything more after this and crosses his arms. I cross my arms back at him and tap my foot under the table. It's not like he can see it but I still do it anyway.

"I'm co-owner." He states simply.

"Co-owner? I'm sure that's a career you could use a college degree for."

He nods slowly in agreeance, "Yes, if that was my career." He sits up looking like he was about to tell the whole story.

"When I came to Tokyo for the first time, I had my brother Ozzy with me. After I handled some business, we were hungry, and Ozzy said it'd be nice if we could find some ice cream somewhere. You know, an ode to our childhood. We walked around what felt like forever until we found the shop that I took you too.

We fell in love instantly and went back twice a day while we were in Japan. After that, it ended up being a tradition of ours to go there. For Ozzy's 18th birthday, I surprised him by buying him 27% ownership into the company. I bought myself 25% because he always said he wanted us to go into business together and this was my way of honoring that.

The owner had no problem with this because he still had 48% of the company in his name and plus, we were bringing in a lot more customers."

Bought ownership? So that means he must've been making money before he even co-owned the shop.

"That's so sweet. You guys must be inseparable." I smile fondly at him.

"Yea, that's my rib. He keeps me going. I'm still trying to figure what to give him for his 21st birthday in a few months." He drifts off into deep thought about this and I make a bold move by rubbing my foot along his shin under the table like he did to me.

He stills and his eyes dart back to me, a dark look in his irises. A look that says if you don't stop now, you'll be devoured on top of this table, no matter who sees.

I clear my throat and start to pull my foot away, but he grabs my ankle with his hand under the table lightly. He brushes his calloused thumb across my ankle gently, the roughness making me shiver with need. I wonder how that roughness will feel on the rest of my body.

"So, let me ask you LG," he says still holding my ankle, his voice showing some grit and roughness to it, giving away that I'm not the only one affected by his touching me. His dark eyes travel up to meet my light, lust filled ones. "What's it like..." his hand grazes up my leg to my calf, and it takes everything in me to not jerk in my seat. "Being in the 1% of people who don't like roller coasters?"

I pull my leg out of his hand and he laughs. I throw a napkin at him and poke my lip out in a pout. "That's not funny."

He grabs his hat and his sunglasses, placing it gracefully on his head and the glasses on his eyes, shutting out the world. He opens the curtains again and waves the waitress over.

She hurries over and they speak in Japanese briefly. Hendi reaches into his back pocket, pulling out his wallet and places a few bills on the table.

"Ready for the next stop?"

Confused at the sudden change of events, I just look at him bewildered.

"Come on, don't chicken out on me now LG." He stands up and steps down from the platformed booth we were sitting at for the past couple of hours. I reluctantly take his hand, not ready to leave the confines of our private booth, but excited to see what else he had in store for our eventful night.

He leads us back out of the building and off into the night towards our next stop in the Tokyo private tour.

Seven

"Let me guess, you plan on breaking into here too." I say as we walk up on the next destination.

The Tokyo Skytree was a building that Theo kept saying he was going to bring me to one night because he said it really was a sight to see. Tonight, the building was illuminated with a beautiful lavender purple color, reminding me of my favorite color lilac. This night really was made for us to meet and explore together.

There are multiple shops decorated along the bottom of the building, in true Tokyo fashion, with lots of outdoor seating for people to use when visiting. Hendrix leads me to the escalators, and we glide up to the second floor.

"It's not breaking in when you have connections LG."

This man must be the president and I was just too behind the times and what's currently going on in the news to know it. The only thing is, what president do you know can easily escape the secret service and wear plaid zipper pants in the process?

I peer up at the Eiffel Tower of Japan and excited jitters flutter through my body.

A buff looking security guard meets us at the top of the escalator and his eyes flicker to me, assessing me and trying to figure me out, before landing back on Hendi's face and softening his features a tad.

"Well well well, if it isn't Mr. Houdini himself. Bruce asked me if I've seen you. You need to call him H."

Bruce?

"You didn't tell him I was coming here did you?" Hendi's jaw ticks and I look back at this security guard that's grilling him. He seems to be slightly annoyed with Hendi and I'm wondering why.

"No, but I *will* if you don't promise you'll call him soon." The guard crosses his arms like he just caught us sneaking into the house late at night.

"Yea yea, just let us inside Grant."

The security guard, Grant, lets out a chuckle and shakes his head softly. He turns around and leads us towards the main entrance of the skytree.

"You have one hour. Make the most of it," he says to Hendi as he holds the door open to us. As I pass by him, I give a little wave and he nods his head toward me in greeting. "Take care of him," Grant says towards me so quietly I think I imagined it.

Shouldn't it be the other way around? Shouldn't I be the one needing protecting since he seems to know everyone under the sun? He might be the son to a powerful mafia boss somewhere.

"Sorry about that," Hendi grits out through his teeth. I rub his bicep to soothe some of the tension that seems to have snuck its way through the doors before Grant closed them.

"Why are you sorry?" I ask, trying not to get distracted by the sculpting of his arm. His bicep was so muscular, and I wondered what the rest of his body looked like. "What was that about anyway?"

"I'll tell you later. For now, I want us to just focus on this night and not the outside world."

I nod in understanding as he guides me towards the elevators. Once inside the car, he pushes the button for the top floor…the 29th floor.

"You excited?" Hendi smiles down at me, a bad boy smirk playing across his face.

"Why do you ask?" I smirk back showing I wasn't intimidated, even though I was.

"Well, you're fidgeting all over the place and can't sit still."

"Maybe I have to pee *Hendrix*," I clip back at him, "I've only been to the bathroom once since we've been together."

The elevator dings and the doors open. I walk off first, looking left and right. The view from where we were was gorgeous. I walk up to the railing and stare at the Tokyo skylight. I just wish there wasn't a glass window blocking me from feeling the cool night from this height.

"You would've told me you had to pee," He walks up to stand beside me, both of his hands in his pockets. This man thinking he has me figured out makes me want to show him that he doesn't in fact know me like that.

"Actually, I do need to use the bathroom. Where is it?"

He eyes me suspiciously before leading me toward the restrooms. I walk in and take this time to assess myself in the mirror. The little bit of eyeliner I put on is still intact which is good, but my face is starting to look oily. I pull my blotch sheets out from my purse and dab at my nose and upper lip. I'm not one of those girls that puts makeup on their face every day, not that its anything wrong with that, it's just not me. After fixing my hair a little and approving of how I look, I mock flush the toilet and wash my hands.

Hendi waits for me, leaning against the wall directly to the left of the restroom door.

"Good?" He raises his eyebrow at me in amusement.

"Yep." I flash him my teeth and he does the same in response.

"Perfect, let's go."

He grabs my hand and interlaces our fingers in an intimate gesture. I'm glad I'm behind him so he can't see the blush that floods my cheeks.

We approach a door that reads **CERTIFIED PERSONNEL ONLY** and of course, Hendi produces a key and unlocks it. On the other side of the door is a ladder that seems to lead us to an even higher spot on the tower.

"Um…is this safe?" my anxiety peeking around a corner as if I called its name.

"Was following around a complete stranger at night safe?" He challenges me and I have nothing to say to that. "I'll go up first and open that hatch, then you'll follow behind me."

He does just this and when he opens the latch, the sounds of the outside night activities fill my ears. His shirt blows a little as the breeze catches it in its grasp, probably eager to feel on his abs like me.

Once he's through the hatch, he bends down and reaches his hand back through to help me up. I walk towards the ladder, the cold metal a contrast to the warmth of my skin. I start up the ladder and when

I get to the point of his hand, I gladly take it and he pulls me up the rest of the way.

"Wow," I say as I take in the breathtaking view from this secret spot on the tower.

"Beautiful isn't it," Hendi's voice fills my ear from the side but I'm still taken aback by the view.

It was something out of a movie. The lights of the city making Tokyo seem like one big Christmas tree. Off in the far distance I could see the other popular tower in Japan, the Tokyo Tower. I wonder if I told Hendi that I wanted to go there, if he'd be able to pull it off like he did this one. He probably will since he had so many connections it seemed.

I turn from the view in front of me to face Hendi and see that he's taken a seat by the hatch. I follow suit, sitting close to him but not too close to where he's uncomfortable. We stare at the view together when this gnawing question that's been on my mind releases itself.

"So…is you knowing Grant the connection that got us into this place?"

"Actually, no. It took a lot of bribing on my end to the owner." He pulls his phone from his pocket and waves it to show me. So, every time he was texting or playing around on his phone, he was setting up for our next destination. Nice to know.

"He almost didn't let us do it until he asked If I could send his daughter a happy birthday video in exchange." He shrugged like it was nothing.

"A happy birthday video? That's it?" Now I feel like I need to pull my phone out to google this man because he must really be a big deal if a simple happy birthday video can get us into a popular landmark way past business hours.

"What can I say LG? I'm a hot commodity." I give his shoulder a light push and he laughs, acting as if I pushed him ten times harder.

We settle back into our comfortable silence and stare out into the view in front of us.

"You know," I say breaking the silence, "this view kind of reminds me of Titanic." I turn to him, and he has a disgusted look on his face. "What? That's a classic movie. One of my favorites."

"A favorite? I don't know if we can continue this night. You're not the person I thought you were." I laugh at the disgust that's etched on his face.

"I'm guessing you're not a fan," I manage to get out over my laughter.

"Don't get me wrong, it was cool for what it was. But there were *so* many questionable things about that movie," he turns his body to where he's facing me so he can emphasis his points. "For example, why is it that a glacier big enough to sink the Titanic, wasn't in view until they were right up on it."

I actually think about this. He has a point.

"Second example. Rose and Jack could've fit on that door together. There was more than enough room for him, but no, she wanted to be selfish."

"Actually," I put my hand up to interject, "They tried to see if they both could fit, and it didn't work."

"She was taking up the whole space and only gave him room on the *edge* of the door to try. Of course it wasn't going to work that way."

I shake my head at him, smiling. "Okay, all of that aside. It was a great movie."

"Yea it's cool, but I like paying attention to the little details. That's how you get far in life LG."

"Anyway," I turn the conversation back to my original point, "Like I was saying, the view reminds me of Titanic. It makes me feel like I'm in Rose's place when she was standing on the edge of the ship."

A lightbulb seems to go off in his mind by the way he smiles at me.

"Want to reenact it?" He asks.

"Are you crazy?" My eyes grow so big, I'm surprised they don't fly me away.

"Only when I'm with you," he says in a joking tone, but something tells me there's some truth to his words.

Ditto Hendi. Ditto.

"How would we reenact that anyway?"

Butterflies escape from their cocoons and wreak havoc in my lower belly. He stands up, adjusts his pants then walks a few steps to the small railing that encompasses us on our private viewing balcony. He curls his index finger towards me, beckoning me to come to him and I do.

As I get closer, my steps slow, and I make the mistake of peering over the edge to look down at the small lights of passing cars and wished I was on the safe ground with them.

Hendi grasps my hand lightly and guides me to stand in the space between him and the balcony in front of us. When I'm standing in front of him, my heart seems to stop while I feel his beating faster in his chest.

"Step up on the bottom of the railing and stretch your arms out," He says into my neck, causing goosebumps to skate down my back.

I shake my head furiously telling him no without words, and he just chuckles behind me. I knew this man was crazy, but I never thought he'd be this crazy. He must be trying to throw me over the edge.

"So… you're scared of roller coasters *and* heights. Got it." He nods curtly behind me and annoyance trickles its way into my blood.

"I'm not scared of heights, I'm scared of falling to my death. There's a difference *Hendrix*." I say his name in a condescending tone to display my annoyance.

He chuckles again, "Don't worry LG, I got you. Just trust me."

Even though I just met this man a few hours ago, something inside me pulls toward his words, and tells me it's okay to trust him.

So, I do.

Stepping up onto the bottom of the railing causes my heart to wake itself back up and pump harder than it's ever pumped before. Hendi places both hands firmly on my hips to ensure that I don't fall over.

I release the ironclad grip I had on the railing and slowly stretch my arms out to the side. His right-hand glides up my stomach and stays on my rib cage to help me feel even more secure. The tips of his fingers brush against the small cup of my right under-boob and I shudder. Luckily, there was a breeze so Hendi would think that was the reason I was trembling in his presence.

I felt like I was flying and falling at the same time. Flying through the crisp Tokyo air, making friends with the birds in the sky and high fiving the stars.

But I also felt like my heart was falling into uncharted waters.

Falling to its death.

Falling where it doesn't belong.

After a few minutes of closing my eyes and imagining soaring through the clouds, I place my hands back at my side to indicate that I'm ready to be let down. He pulls me off the railing, letting my back slowly slide against his hard, muscular front, my dress raising up in the process. I pass over a bulge in his pants and sparks shoot through the space between my thighs, as if being awakened after an eternity of slumber. He pulls my dress back down, his knuckles skating across the warm, heated skin on my hips.

I wish we had more than one night together just so I can fulfill the fantasies playing out in my head right now. I wish we met on different circumstances and I wish that I knew more about him.

If this magical night could conjure up a shooting star, that'd be perfect.

"How was that?" His gruff voice whispers into my ear as he leans down from where he's standing behind me. The gravelly tone of his voice is like an energy shot to my core.

"Magical," is all I manage to breathe out while I attempt to reel in my self-control.

"Come on. I want to take you to the most magical place in the world."

"Wait, can we just stare at the view a little longer?" It doesn't skip by me that he's still holding me from behind, our bodies glued together like that's where they're meant to be.

"We can do whatever you want." He says sweetly. That statement is ironic because really, we've been doing what he *thinks* I'll want this whole night. I'm not complaining though.

We stand like this, my back to his front, staring off into the distance, soaking in the beauty of the Tokyo night skyline.

We don't have much time left in the night, and I wonder how many more stops Hendi has planned for us before we bid our goodbyes. I stop thinking about it because a sense of loss starts to clog my throat and stirs up sadness in my gut.

Hendi…what are you doing to me?

Eight

"Voila! The best place on Earth," He extends his arms like a showman displaying a new exotic car he just got in the lot.

"A music store?" Confusion is etched in my voice as he just looks at me nodding, with the biggest smile I've ever seen on his face.

"Come on," He walks into the still open store excitedly. "Tonight, they're having one of their 24-hour special days, so we won't have the shop to ourselves. That's okay though."

Even though the place was open, it still felt empty because of there only being two other people in the store. It wasn't by any means empty in terms of the instruments they had to offer. In fact, different types of guitars decorated every surface available in this building.

"I've never seen so many guitars in one place before," I say in awe, walking around and taking it all in.

"Beautiful isn't it?" He asks as he sets his sights on one guitar in particular and fingers its strings. It was an acoustic guitar with a dark red finish and yellow accents, almost reminding me of a gala apple. It was gorgeous.

He grabs it off the hook it's hanging on and walks over to one of the white comfy accent chairs by the glass display case. I follow him and take a seat in the one beside his.

"You play?" I ask, watching him turn the pegs on the head of the guitar.

"You can say that. I mostly play electric now, but whenever I get the chance, I like to channel back to my roots and have fun with an acoustic."

He starts playing some wonky sounding notes and turning the pegs at the same time until it seems like he's got the sound he was looking for. He plays around with popular songs, only playing little snippets before jumping to the next song. I clap for him and encourage him to keep going.

He gives me a nervous smile, making him look 10 years younger than he is and it melts my heart. He breathes out a long-resigned breath before he starts playing again.

A sad, sorrowful tune bleeds out of the guitar, stealing my breath away. I'm scared to breathe, move, or even blink because I don't want anything to take away this feeling. I'm entranced. Hendi gets lost in the song he's playing, and his face scrunches up in concentration. His body seems to dance with the guitar, and they move across the floor in a powerful waltz that demands everyone's attention. I eventually close my eyes and find myself lost in his song, a story starting to form in my ears and emotions riding along the soundwaves in the room.

I get a glimpse into his struggles and the battle of emotions that's taking place in his head. I get a sense of why he needed this night to escape. I get the overwhelming feeling of wanting to take all his pain away so his sad song can morph from a melancholic melody into a euphoric symphony.

And then it stops.

I feel like a rug has been ripped out from under my feet. My eyes shoot open and I see Hendi staring at me intently.

I clear my throat and look everywhere but at him because not only do I feel as though I've been stripped naked, the feeling I get from his gaze makes me feel even more bare. It's as though his eyes weren't being blocked by his dark shades and he wasn't hiding from the world.

"That was… I—" I start to say but my words fall short. I don't even know how to describe what I just experienced. "I can see why you call this the best place on Earth." I finally spit out.

He stands up and places the guitar back on its hook before walking towards a door at the back of the shop. He holds it open for me as I stand up and walk through it, greeted by more instruments. This room is two times bigger than the one we were just in and it houses instruments ranging from pianos, to cellos to even musical triangles.

"You're really good at guitar," I say to Hendi when he stands to the side of me. He rubs the back of his neck and gives a shy smile.

"Thank you. I've been playing it since I was young."

"How'd you learn?" I walk over to the pianos and wonder if he knows how to play those too. He follows behind me and stops a couple feet away.

"I learned from watching my Dad play. When he realized I was interested, he started to teach me." He places his hands in his pocket and watches me as I glide my finger along the keys of a lone keyboard in the corner of the room.

I turn so my whole body is facing the keys, giving me all the comfort I need to start playing. I play the only song I know, which coincidentally, is the only song I've ever cared to learn.

I take a seat on the bench and press my fingers down onto the black and white keys. My left hand taking over the base of the song while my right hand sings its solo and brings back a flood of memories. My eyes shutter closed, as if I've been possessed by the ghosts of my past. The emptiness that's stained in my heart suffocates me and reminds me of what this song has meant to me. I haven't played this song in years.

Not since that day.

My brows furrow as my body rocks back and forth, my face tightening as I start to feel the keys and attempt to control the emotions that are spilling over at the same time. I know exactly how Hendi feels when he plays the guitar because I feel the same when I play the piano.

As I'm halfway through the song, I'm pulled out of the depths of my subconscious as I feel Hendrix move behind me and take a seat on the bench next to me. I don't stop playing nor do I open my eyes because it's important that I finish. I need to give him a look into my mind the same way he did me. I just hope he really *sees* me.

Then I hear it. He places his hands on the keys, making sure he's not in the way of mine, and adds his own little twist to the song, creating a powerful duet. We move together and the private song that I've cherished for so many years becomes even more perfect in a matter of seconds. I never thought it was possible.

The song comes to an end and as the final key drags out into the air, I let out a shaky breath and nod my head to myself in acceptance.

As I open my eyes, loud applause fills the room and I'm shocked at the sight in front of me. Like magic, the huge music room went from being occupied by four people, to what looked like 60. They all whistled and hollered, raving about Hendi and I's impromptu performance.

I turn to Hendi and realize he took off his shades. The look in his eyes is chilling. It looks as though he's a lion who's just surrounded their prey and is about to go in for the kill. His Adams apple bobs as he swallows and his tongue darts out to lick his lips.

"Do you realize how perfect you are?" He looks confused as he asks me this, as if he can't believe it himself.

Just as I open my mouth to respond, yells come from the crowd of applause.

"Hendi is that you!?"

"OMG IT'S HENDI!"

"CAN I GET A PICTURE?"

"Is she your girlfriend!?"

"SIGN MY BOOBS!?"

Numerous flashes of light start to hit us as we're blinded by paparazzi cameras.

"Shit," Hendi hisses next to me and shoots up from the bench. An older looking man with strings of hair draped across his bald head runs up to us and says something in Japanese.

"Come on LG. We need to get out of here." He extends his hand to me and I gladly take it. He ushers me in front of him so that he's blocking me from the mayhem that appeared out of nowhere. The old man leads us to a backroom and holds the door open for us as he motions his hand for us to hurry inside.

Nine

The room we were now in shut out all the noise and commotion from outside. It was small with no windows and a black leather love seat against the wall. It looked like it was used to give music lessons.

I sit down trying to wrap my brain around what the hell just happened, while Hendi paces back and forth within our small confines.

After a couple of minutes, he stops, and a smirk plays across his face. "Beethoven. Great choice, although, I didn't expect Moonlight Sonata to be the sound that came out." His hands are on his hips and his head is tilted to the side as if he's trying to figure me out when really it should be the other way around.

I need to be figuring him out and fast.

"Don't try to ignore the fact that we got bombarded by people who seem to care about you *a lot*." His face turns red in a surprise blush that squeezes my heart. Was he shy? Nervous?

"So, you saw that huh?" He jerks his thumb towards the door, in the direction of the crowd.

I give him a stern look and he raises his hands up in defeat. He walks over and takes a seat next to me, sucking in a deep breath.

"Are you ready to tell me what it is you do or are you still going to make me guess?"

He lets out a long breath, scrubbing his eyes under his sunglasses that he slipped back on with his right hand. I don't see the point in the disguise anymore seeing as we've been caught. He's leaning forward onto his knees and doesn't look at me.

"I'm a porn star."

If I had water in my mouth, it'd be flying all over the room, but mostly into the side of his face. My eyes shoot up in horror and agony starts to form in the pit of my stomach. Is that why that lady wanted him to sign her boobs? Because she's seen how skilled his hands were. I knew I noticed tremendous skill when he was playing the guitar.

A loud roar of laughter punches me from where he sits. He's thrown himself back into the couch and a lone tear strolls down towards his ear. I punch him hard in his rib and he doesn't even flinch.

His torso is rock hard, and his ab muscles are like shock absorbers. He wipes his eyes then sits back up smiling at me. My face goes from horrified to annoyed in less than a minute.

"Ok, ok. I'm sorry." He wipes his hands on his pants then shakes his head, getting the last of his laughter out. "I'm a musician. A tad bit well known to some."

I give a sarcastic smile, failing to believe he's only a *tad bit* well known.

"Only a tad bit? So why were you chased down by that mob of girls earlier tonight?"

"The little fans I have tend to be a little on the crazy side. That just means they're more passionate." He winks at me and it makes my skin crawl deliciously.

"I figured you were a musician right when you started playing that guitar out there. When you add the cliché Rockstar look, the tattoos and the musical talent, it doesn't take much to figure out the answer. I was just waiting for you to admit it."

He scoots closer to me on the couch so that he's now sitting in the middle instead of the opposite end as me.

"I knew you were a smart girl and that you'd figure it out eventually. I just wanted one night of peace with genuine, honest company. Is that too much to ask for?"

"What makes you think that if you told me from the beginning that I wouldn't be genuine and honest?"

He mulls over his response before carefully saying his next words.

"Meeting girls who don't know who I am is hard to come by. They usually throw themselves at me and fake interest in anything that I do besides music, just so they can be paraded on my arm. There are also girls who fake like they don't know me but come to find out they're the leader of a secret Hendi lovers society."

I shake my head.

"Bottom line is, even though I could tell you genuinely didn't know who I was, I didn't want to risk saying something that'd jog your memory and cause you to realize you actually *do* know me and that I made one of your favorite songs or something."

A tad bit well known huh?

"So…If I were to figure out who you were earlier, you would've ended the tour?"

He thinks on this, rubbing his chin stubble, creating a gravelly noise.

"No. You're different from the rest LG and I'm curious about you. Curious as to why you know and bare pain, curious as to why you seek adventure, and curious as to why you willingly put your trust into a complete stranger. It's strange for me to admit, but I want to know more about you."

His nostrils flare and he breathes air down his face. "I can't believe I just said that," he mumbles.

"What do you mean?" I ask wishing he'd stop being such a mystery to me. He shakes his head not giving me the answers I want. I try a different tactic.

"Okay. What made you choose music?" I cross my legs and lean back into the couch, getting comfortable.

"That'd be my dad again. Growing up, I remember him always wanting to be a famous guitarist. He idolized Jimi Hendrix and Ozzy Osbourne, which is why he named his only children after them." I let out a giggle that causes him to pause his story and look at me with a sinful grin.

I motion for him to continue and I almost think he doesn't, but in true Hendi fashion, he surprises me.

"I would always sneak and watch him play during the night when I was supposed to be sleeping. He would go outside on the porch at like 3:00 am and just strum to himself. It was something about the music that captivated me."

He swallows hard as he remembers his past.

"One night I got caught, and he told me to pull up a chair. He started to teach me things here and there and would explain just how important music was to the world. He said *'Son, Music is an outlet that allows lost souls to find themselves, even if it's just for a little bit.'"*

He takes off his hat and sunglasses, scrubbing his hand over his face. A sad smile is plastered on his now boyish looking features.

"Wow, he must be an amazing person," I offer, hoping I'm not way off base.

"Yeah…yeah, he was."

Was.

His choice of words doesn't escape me, and my next question almost doesn't come out. It's trapped under the mass of hurt I feel for the man sitting in front of me.

What have you been through Hendi?

"Do you…do you think you play music for you or for him?"

He sits there for a long minute without saying a word. I inwardly punch myself for prodding too much. Obviously, it's hard for him to talk about what he went through as a child. I can only imagine the amount of heartbreak he's had to endure.

Eventually he stands up and heads towards a door at the back of the room that reads emergency exit.

"I think we've been hiding away long enough. It should be safe to head to the next destination now."

I feel weird just leaving things how they were and having this awkward tension between us.

"Look Hendi, I'm sor---"

"Don't worry about it LG. It's nothing. Now come on before all the good seats are taken."

Ten

"Sumo wrestling!?" I jump up and down squealing as we walk into a building that resembles a mall. There's a cardboard cutout of sumo wrestlers to my right as Hendi guides us to where we need to be.

"You excited?" he smirks down at me and I don't care that I look like a little kid. Watching a sumo wrestling match was something I've always subconsciously wanted to do but didn't realize I wanted it this bad.

"Watching men wrestling around in thongs is my favorite pass time," I joke, finally finishing my excited jumps. We walk up to a man at a side door and Hendi produces two tickets he bought out front, allowing us access to the main event. The man nods in approval towards us and opens the doors.

We walk into what appears to be a stadium with a platform down below made of hardened clay, a circle outlined in the middle to signal that it's the appointed wrestling ring. The seats that are down closer to the platform are just comfy mats laid out on the floor and as you go higher up in level, they eventually transform into cushiony mahogany colored seats with back support.

"Which would you rather do? Sit close and get the full experience, or sit up top so we can talk shit to each other and bet on our favorite sumo?" He nudges me lightly in the ribs, pulling me away from my assessment of the place.

"The latter sounds way more fun," I wink up at him and nudge him back.

I like that his playful mode made a full recovery after that awkward moment in the music room. I wonder if I'll be able to get any more information out of him tonight.

Hendi starts walking up towards the top and decides on some seats that are not too far back, but far away from the front. There aren't many people in here yet, but they quickly start to file in once we get comfortable.

"Have you been to one of these before?" I whisper in his ear as a couple takes a seat beside me. I'm sure he's been to one of these countless times seeing as he knew about it and basically had connections to every nook and cranny in this city.

He shakes his head while hitching one shoulder up. "Actually, no. I've always wanted to go, but my schedule would conflict whenever there was a match."

My eyebrows shoot up in surprise. "How'd you know about the match tonight?"

"When we were walking to Joypolis, I saw a sign posted on one of the ramen bars nearby. I decided I had to work it into our schedule and felt like it'd be something you'd enjoy." He leans into me, giving a half smile. "My gut is never wrong." He flicks my nose lightly and I let out a loud snort.

Covering my mouth in horror, I look to him hoping he didn't hear it.

"Whoa, what was that?" He laughs.

Shit.

"I do that sometimes if I laugh when I'm nervous. I hate it."

"I think it's cute," He leans his shoulder against mine and stays there.

A loud noise bangs through our quiet moment from the platform below, and I look to see a slim older looking man playing the bongos. That signals that they're ready to start the main event. Still, Hendi doesn't disconnect from where our bodies are touching.

A small skinny woman in a kimono walks onto the platform waving a colorful fan. She twirls it around in the air in a circular motion before saying something in Japanese. She signals for the first two fighters to come up and I immediately know the fighter I'm going to root for.

The fighter to the right is about 60 lbs. lighter than the fighter on the left, so much so that I wouldn't even consider him sumo. I can almost see his abs poking through the small layer of fat on top. The fighter on the right, however, looks so squishy and had rolls that made me want to squeeze them like a stress ball.

Is that weird?

They both sport black colored sumo thongs, showing off their asses and I wonder if Hendi avoids making contact with their cheeks or if he doesn't care and just watches all aspects of the men as they take their spots in their respective corners.

"Who're you placing your bets on, LG?" Hendi whispers towards me but keeps his eyes on the ring.

"I got SSW," I say simply, happy with my choice.

"SSW?" He finally turns his head to me, and I'm hating he still has to keep his disguise on. I want to be able to bask in his beauty without barriers.

"Yea, Skinny Sumo Wrestler, duh." He shakes his head at me.

"I thought you'd go for BCG."

"BCG?" I quirk an eyebrow playfully.

"Yea, Big Chunky Guy."

It isn't until the lady in the middle waves her fan at the wrestlers and they start squatting and waving their arms in unison, that I realize we didn't even say what we were betting. I shrug it off though, and just wait for Hendi to say something about it. Right now, I'm too fascinated at what's taking place a few feet below me to care.

"I'm not the kind of girl who is predictable by the way. Despite how many hits you have tonight compared to your misses." I whisper shout to him and the couple next to me shushes me. I didn't know you had to be quiet at a Sumo wrestling match.

"And exactly how *many* misses do I have *Ariana?*"

I shudder at the sound of my name on his tongue and shake my head.

Clowns. Holes. Spiders. Bunnies.

I list all the things I'm scared of to keep from letting the desire in my lower core ache and leak all over my cushioned seat. (Have you actually looked at a bunny before? Like *really* looked at it? Evil little things. Don't be fooled).

I'm not ready to give into whatever this thick tension is between us. Not ready to end this night.

"Shh, it's starting." Is all I say in response to his question because I didn't want to inflate his ego by telling him he hasn't missed yet.

"GET HIM! YES! GO SSW!" I'm screaming my lungs off to my fighter and don't care what anyone else thinks. I feel like I'm his coach and I'm standing on the edge of the ring, willing him to pull through for the win.

By some miracle, SSW manages to trip BCG, causing him to fall to the ring with a loud thud, making SSW the winner of the match. It was a close match, and I started to sweat after the third round, but he really proved me right.

Don't ever judge a book by its cover or underestimate it.

Hendi is laughing so hard at the fact I screamed like a mad man, that his hat fell off and his beautiful hair is tousled in every direction. I smile hard at him from where I'm standing up and kick him lightly in the leg.

"I win, what do I get?"

He runs his hand through his hair, collecting himself and readjusts his crooked sunglasses. My eyes shift to the women around us who just stare at him with their mouth agape, even the lady with the man sitting next to us. Yea yea, I know, he's beautiful. He gets to me too.

"Well…for one, I didn't expect for you to be so into it," He grabs my wrist and tugs on it so that I'm pulled down to sit across him. Not exactly in his lap, but my legs are draped over his thighs, and my butt sits against the outside of his thigh. "But you, my dear LG, are now blessed with the gift of choice."

I clap my hands excitedly. "I get to choose where we go next?" my smile so prominent on my face, you'd think I was getting a checkup at the dentist.

"Not that big of a choice I'm afraid. 1 or 2? Choose wisely."

My face falls at the fact I can't take him somewhere I found in my short time here, but I'm buzzing with anxious energy to know what's behind door number 1 and 2.

"Do I get a hint?" I have a hopeful gleam in my eye.

"One is even, and one is odd." I swat his chest and he chuckles. "Just choose. Go with what your gut is telling you."

My brain is telling me to go for two because I'm a sucker for even numbers, but my gut is telling me one was chosen as number one for a reason.

"One," I finally say after tapping my chin in thought for what feels like a long minute.

"Finally. I was starting to fall asleep." He places one of his arms under the bend in my knees and another hooked around my back. He stands up with me in his arms, shocking me with the amount of strain he isn't in from lifting us both up with just the strength in his legs.

We look like a couple who'd just gotten married and he was carrying me over the threshold. I grabbed his hat on the way up from the ground and placed it back neatly on his beautiful mane.

"Can't forget the disguise," I flush at how close our faces are when he turns to look at me. His gaze shifts down to my lips and I instinctively dart my tongue out to lick them, afraid they look dry. I taste the cherry Chapstick I applied after the vampire dinner and bite down on my lower lip nervously. His eyes grow dark with something primal in them, and his eyelids lower just a tad. Our lips are so close that if I even lean forward an inch, they'd be touching.

I wonder if his are as soft and strong as I'm imagining in my head. I wonder what kind of kisser he is. Does he dominate and control it, telling my tongue where he wants it to go, or does he make it an equal effort and lets me dominate for a little?

Maybe if I move a little closer…

He clears his throat and I'm instantly snapped back to reality. He places me down on the ground and puts his hands in his pockets. I straighten my dress and pick up my purse from the ground.

"You ready?" He asks, looking everywhere but at me, his voice sounding strained like he was trying to hold something back.

"Yep," I say following behind him as he walks out into the main lobby of the building.

"Two waffle cones of vanilla bean please," I say to the ice cream stand worker in the busy alleyway. On our way to our next destination, we were having casual conversation about what my time in Tokyo has been like so far. I told him about my coworkers and how they butt heads with each other a lot on certain studies.

We ended up passing by an ice cream vendor and I decided to stop, thinking it'd be good to get Hendi some sweets. I wanted to make up for the awkward conversation in the music room and whatever the hell happened after the sumo show. I know his pallet is more elite and has seen more outlandish ice cream flavors, but I just wanted him to have something normal seeing as his life is anything but.

I pull out my wallet and start trying to pay when Hendi puts his hand on mine to stop me. "Let me. I'm the one in charge of this tour." He reaches into his back pocket to pull out his wallet, but I rush and pull out my bills, placing them in the vendor's hand.

"Don't worry about it," I turn to him after taking both cones in my hand. "You've been footing the bill this whole time, I wanted to do this for you at least. Besides, this ice cream was my idea."

I hand him his waffle cone and he reluctantly takes it from me. He raises his eyebrow in question at the flavor I chose, and I almost didn't answer but decided better of it.

"I decided you needed some normalcy in your life, and you can never go wrong with vanilla." He stares at me for a moment, then nods in agreement and we continue our walk to our next destination.

After what felt like long moments of goofing around, racing each other to a light pole, and trying to guess people's life stories, we approach one of the most unique things I've seen tonight. He points to a bench under a flowing tree for us to sit and get a perfect view of this beautiful scenery.

Eleven

"Welcome to Rainbow Bridge. Adding to the color that is Tokyo." Hendi points to the bridge just in case I couldn't see it, even though it was the only thing in front of me.

Its pillars were lit up in a beautiful rainbow assortment of orange, yellow, green, blue and purple. The rest of the bridge was illuminated in the green color and the lights of the passing cars made it seem like I was looking at a moving painting. Absolutely stunning. If you add in the view of the river, it seems like one of those places you'd see in the movies when a bride runs away from her groom.

Ships sail by, probably carrying cargo and other important things needed to keep Japan alive.

"It's beautiful," I breathe out, leaning back into the bench, loving my life right now. It's like I'm having an elaborate lucid dream and suddenly I'll be woken up and this perfect night will be snatched up from beneath me.

"I figured you'd like it, and since you're a colorful person, this seemed like the perfect place to go next."

What does he mean by that? I almost conjured up enough courage to ask, but it instantly shot back down again when he leaned back into the bench and draped his arms along the back of it.

His thumb absentmindedly rubs against my shoulder as if it's been doing it for many years. The one thing I love about hanging with Hendi is the sense of comfortability and familiarity I get from him. I feel as though he's a childhood friend I've had a crush on since I was in diapers. Maybe that's why I've been so willing to follow him around and share pieces of myself I wouldn't normally share so quickly.

I wonder if he feels the same about me.

"What kind of musician are you?" I turn my attention away from the bridge and glance at him to my left. I craved more information about him so the pieces that were falling into place would be glued together, and I'll finally know Hendrix in his entirety.

"I'm in a band. I'm the lead singer and songwriter of the group. I guess you could compare our music to be more like a mix of Blink 182, Maroon 5, and Queen."

"So you're a Rockstar. Cool. What's your band's name?"

"Heart Failure. And we don't really stick to one genre, we just make whatever music hits our souls."

"Why heart failure?" Lots of bands have very unique names that have deeper meanings and I'm sure theirs was no exception.

"Every member of the band has been through some trying times that's caused our hearts to not beat the same. It seemed fitting." I didn't expect such a sad explanation. I figured he'd say that they cause women's hearts to stop with their beautiful faces and voices. I'm still surprised I didn't guess Rockstar as his secret profession earlier.

This explains the flock of fan girls and connections. But I'm sure I would've seen him or heard of him before since he's so "famous".

"How many of you are there?" I've never met a Rockstar before, and I'm honestly surprised I'm crossing off so many things form my invisible bucket list in one night.

"4 of us in total. My brother joined the band when he turned 16. At that time, we were getting a little buzz and record labels wanted to talk business."

"Why is it that I've never heard of you before? What's one of your most popular songs?"

He seems as though he's trying to pick from a long list of songs in his head before a light bulb flashes and he decides on one. He starts humming a familiar tune, then opens his mouth to sing and the sound of his rough, raspy singing voice fills my ears. He sings about losing a precious love and how he's searched all over the world to find that person again just to get closure, but all they give is their back to his desperate pleas. I instantly recognize the song as the one Theo, my best friend, was obsessed with for months a few years ago. He played it nonstop and raved about this band, but I never took the time out to give them a listen.

"I've heard that song before. Of course it was you," I shake my head smiling at the way the world works.

"What do you mean of course? And do you like the song?" He looks like a little boy waiting for approval from his parent.

"Of course you'd be the famous singer I heard nonstop every day for months on end. And the song is beautifully heartbreaking, which I'm sure is the tone you were going for. Who was the inspiration?"

"It's about my dad." He takes off his shades and hat, running his hand through his hair before scrubbing it down his face. He looks sad all over again and I don't want us to go back to that awkward state from earlier.

"Wow. It's amazing though." I offer him comfort by reaching up and squeezing the hand that holds the thumb that was lazily rubbing my shoulder.

"Thank you. Music is an important outlet for me. When everything gets crazy and I feel like I need to scream, I scream through my music. Not literally, but through the words." I nod in understanding and the sadness on his faces passes faster than it showed up.

"I'm guessing Rockstar life isn't all roses and daisies huh?"

He gives a warm chuckle and I lean in closer to him on instinct. His body heat radiates toward me and he even scoots closer to me so I can be more comfortable.

"It gets overwhelming. That's why whenever I get the opportunity, I sneak off to get some time away from all the noise."

"Is that what happened tonight?" I peer up at him from where I'm laying my head on the inside of his broad shoulder. He looks at me and just nods. I place my head back down thinking that me not looking at him would help him open up more.

"We had a benefit show earlier today and I was going through the motions of press, meet and greets, interviews and blah blah," He waves his hand in the air and I feel the movement of his muscles under my ear. He smells so good, like cinnamon, fresh laundry detergent, and his own unique scent.

"I was physically there but I wasn't mentally there. I decided it was time to take a quick break before people started noticing my emptiness."

I want to know what's eating away at him. He needs to be able to talk to people about how he feels and not just bottle it all in. I wish we had more than one night to show him it's okay to open up even if it seems like the last thing you want to do. I nestle into him more, hoping I can express to him that I'm here for whatever he needs.

"How'd you manage to escape all of that commotion?" I mimic his hand wave before dropping it back down, brushing his thigh on accident. He moves his hips and shifts in his seat, letting out a soft groan that I almost mistake as the winds whispers.

He clears his throat.

"Well…we had just gotten back to the hotel from the last interview of the day. Ozzy and I were sharing a room, per usual, and the other guys went back to their rooms to shower. Ozzy volunteered to shower first and when he got in, I grabbed my wallet and headed towards the door. Our bodyguards were standing in the hall having a conversation and when they saw me, they were quick to question where I 'thought' I was going."

I laugh from my spot on the bench at him thinking he can easily slip through like he isn't a global sensation.

"I told them I wanted to go sit in the coffee shop in the lobby to get some alone time. Bruce, Ozzy and I's personal guard, offered to come with me but I told him I needed to be alone. He wouldn't take no for an answer, so I told him I was trying to find inspiration for our new album. He knew that getting our new album made was top priority for the label and important for our careers. He ended up letting me go alone, and I slipped out the back door of the hotel once I reached the first floor."

"So I've been keeping you from working on your new album?" I sit up and a quick shot of coldness hits the left side of my body that was leaning against his hard, secure frame. He was so warm, it's unnatural.

"Actually, no. I finished the album a couple years ago, a week after the release of our last one." He rubs the back of his neck and gives a lopsided grin.

"Do your band mates know?" I ask him, wondering why he kept it a secret from his label and bodyguards.

"Yea, I'm not a complete asshole. We've been silently working and perfecting it on our own in our house. We all share a band house by the way. We use it to jam out and record albums and other stuff. We all also have our own apartments for when we get tired of each other."

"You all must be really close." I could sense how his mood lightens up when he talks about his bandmates. Almost as much as he lights up when talking about his baby brother.

"They're my family. Bruce is too, but some things I keep from him because he gets overprotective."

I lean back into him, listening to the steadiness of his heartbeat and matching it with the calmness of the flowing water, and the brightness of the Rainbow Bridge. He had people around him that clearly cared and loved him, he had his brother, a career that others could only dream of, so I wonder what's eating away at him and why.

Was the way he grew up still haunting him? Was he lost in the shadows of his past? What would it take to free him?

Now I know, after this night is over, I'm going to go listen to all the music they've ever released to hear his cries for help. Hear the story behind this insanely gorgeous man. Hear Hendrix Evans and not just Hendi.

I realized he was sharing with me who he was, offering information somewhat comfortably, but I had yet to share with him who I was. I decided to start with why I wanted to get into brain research in the first place.

Twelve

"Thank you for sharing a piece of you with a total stranger." I offer jokingly.

"Eh, I wouldn't consider you a stranger anymore LG. You're basically at associate status," He twirls a lock of my hair around his right forefinger. My scalp tingles at the attention and I hope my hair didn't look too crazy from the adventures we'd had.

I playfully roll my eyes even though he can't see my face from this angle.

"Whatever," I say, and he laughs. "Anyway, since you're sharing so much, I feel weird not sharing anything about myself."

"It *would* be nice to know more about you…"

Silence fills our bubble as I try to figure out where to start and what information I feel is important. I guess Hendrix took my silence as a sign that I'm uncomfortable sharing, so he nudges me, causing me to sit up and look him in the eyes.

"Hey," he hooks his finger and lifts my chin, "You don't have to share if you don't want too. It's okay."

I shake my head, "No, I want too." I clear my throat and sit up straighter, attempting to exude confidence and hoping that it's working.

"I want to be a Cognitive Psychologist. I guess that's a good place to start the *Who is Ariana* documentary."

He turns his mouth down and nods his head in approval, "Interesting. I've never heard that before." He sits there for a second before asking, "What is that exactly?"

I giggle and his smile turns predatory, so I quickly start talking again before he gets any ideas.

"Basically, someone who studies the activities of the brain. Most of them work in research centers and research topics such as memory, auditory and visual perception, reasoning, and more." I don't want to bore him with medical terms and the things I would be doing on the daily basis once I get offered a full-time position.

"Right now, I'm an intern at FLEa Tech, but hopefully I'll be offered a full-time position soon."

He claps his hands lightly, smiling at me wide. "Congratulations. I know you'll get that position, you're a firecracker. Why cognitive psychology though? Why are you so interested in the brain?"

Here we go. I have to tell my best and worst memories right at this moment, reliving all the scenes that made me become Ariana. I smile thinking about them and try not to cry as I keep thinking about them. Breathe in. Breathe out. In. Out. Okay.

"My grandfather, Grampy Ned, was the closest person to me growing up. He had so much light in his eyes and would smile so wide when he saw me. When I was about 8 years old, that light started to dim. He started forgetting his name, where he was, who he was, and his own children. It got so bad he couldn't even recognize his own face in the mirror." I applaud myself internally for being able to get that out without choking on my own words. I feel my cheeks to make sure no tears were sliding down without my knowledge.

I don't look at Hendrix because I don't want to see pity on his face, and if I did, I'd break down right here and not finish my story.

"My favorite color has always been lilac and before his 'condition' started, Grampy would always buy me things that color. He made it a challenge to get the most unique thing in lilac and gift it to me for my birthday. It was one of the things I looked forward to the most."

Hendi rubs my back to comfort me and I gulp down the sobs fighting their way up my throat. I clear my throat and continue.

"One day, he was sitting in front of a window, just staring out blankly. He had frequent episodes where his eyes would be completely empty, and he'd just stare at nothing. This particular day I decided to sit with him and hold his hand as he looked out. We would always sit on the porch rocking in our chairs, mine was a smaller version but it still worked the same. Anyway. I pulled up a chair and grabbed his right hand, squeezing it to let him know I was there."

I gave a small smile as I recalled this day and what happened next that shaped my future forever.

"When I squeezed his hand, he turned his head to me and said 'Lily' with recognition on his face. I said 'No, it's Ari' trying not to cry that he still didn't remember me. But then he pointed at the shirt I was wearing, and it was one he bought me for my birthday with lilac flowers all around it. I realized he was trying to say lilac and that he remembered it was my favorite color. I jumped up from my chair so fast, yelling for my parents and they came rushing in."

My smile fell and I don't even fight the tears that stream down my face.

"I thought It was a breakthrough. I thought he was getting better since he could remember something. From that day until has last, he called me Lily every time he saw me, and his eyes would flicker with a small amount of light. A small amount of life, like he was fighting to stay on this earth for me. It wasn't until he collapsed and got put in the hospital that my parents told me he was diagnosed with Alzheimer's Disease."

Hendi brushes the tears from my cheeks, then pulls my hand up to his mouth to kiss it. I still don't look at his face, partly because I'm embarrassed for crying in front of him, but also because I can't see through my tears. I close my eyes for a long while before continuing.

"He left this world a few days after my 9th birthday. I celebrated with him and ended up bringing him a friendship bracelet with lilac charms and his favorite things like a chess piece, because he always loved to let me beat him in chess, a football because he played back in his college years and said it was the third best experience in his life, and other things. I also had a matching one, and when I put his on, he rubbed it and smiled. It was the first time I've seen him smile since his light was dimmed. His last words to me were, 'My Lily Forever'."

I was sobbing now, remembering the beauty of the man I admired, looked up to, and loved. He was and still is my everything. Hendi pulls me into him and lets me soak his black shirt. He continues to rub my back up and down, then in circles, and kisses the crown of my head. After a few minutes, I sit back up and shake my head, attempting to shake the tears out. I wipe my face and clear my throat.

"Um… yea, so…ever since then, I've been curious as to how he wasn't able to remember his own face, but was able to remember the smallest, most unimportant detail like my favorite color. I thought the brain was a unique thing and I wanted an answer to my question, thus Ariana being a Cognitive Psychologist was born."

I finally look at him and what I saw on his face wasn't pity, but mirrored pain. As if he knew exactly how I felt and experienced a similar situation of hurt. I wanted to know more but didn't pry because it wasn't my place, and I knew how it felt when people did that.

I tap my chin and try to figure out what direction to go in next with my story and opt to talk about my parents.

"My dad decided to open a picture frame shop in Manhattan because he felt like it was important to have a beautiful frame to accompany beautifully captured memories. He got this idea because the frames we had with pictures of my Grampy weren't *adequate* enough."

"For the first few years, his business was doing okay, enough to stay open but then it started going downhill. He started losing more money than he was earning, and I felt guilty because I wasn't able to help. I started working a few odd jobs while I was in school so I could help them with the bills, but he always turned me down. I tried so hard not to be a burden and he would emphasize that I wasn't, but I still felt like I was. I also didn't want to see the business that he started in honor of Grampy's life crumble to the ground, but there was nothing I could do."

"I'm almost positive you weren't a burden. I'm sure they were glad to help you and give you all the resources you need." Hendi finally speaks up for the first time since I started, and his soothing raspy voice fills me with a much-needed comfort.

"I mean this in the nicest way possible, but…how would you know?"

"You're basically saying you felt like you were a burden just from being a daughter. I'm telling you, they never saw you as anything more than their perfect daughter. Were you a bad, unruly kid?" He quirks a brow up at me.

"No."

"Okay then. Stop saying you were a burden. Case closed."

"Fine," I cross my arms and pout because I feel like a little kid that's just been put in my place by an adult.

"Well, that's the story of me and why I'm obsessed with brains. Maybe I'll do some undercover research on you in the future." Wiggling my brows, I lean forward toward him and he shakes his head.

"You can try, but I'll sue. Hope you have the funds LG."

I swat his chest and turn back to the view, falling into his side, mimicking how I was laying earlier. We watch the traffic on the bridge and the cargo ships going by underneath. I point to one of the far left, alone far away from the bridge.

"What do you think's in that ship?" I ask him and he turns his head to see which one I'm pointing at.

"Cocaine." He stated simply like he knew for a fact.

"You must be a drug pin on the side or something. That must be your shipment."

"Wow. You're so good at guessing what I do for a living." He stands up from the bench and I'm sad at the sudden loss of his warmth.

"C'mon LG. Our time limit for the tour is almost over and we still have two more stops." I push myself up off the bench and fall into stride beside him as we walk.

Thirteen

"What is this place?" I asked as we walked up to a huge statue. It was made of what looked like bronze and it was a group of men in baggy, robed clothing, all in different poses sharing different facial expressions. They were probably created to show the different emotions going on in the time they were made to depict.

It was hard to tell what the building was because there were no signs or anything besides the statue to give me hints. Hendi had put his hat back on during our walk here but didn't put the sunglasses on since it was late, and he didn't think anyone would be out to really recognize him. He just pulled his hat down low and surprisingly, it worked.

"The National Museum of Western Art. I'm not sure if you're an art person, but I'm a sucker for beautiful paintings and sculptures." He looked almost shy and hopeful that I'd like this place. I've never been to a legit art museum before, but I've always wanted to go. Always envisioned myself at some fancy art gallery with a wine glass in my right hand, and my left hand hooked around my date's bicep as we glided across the room.

"I've always wanted to act posh and say art terms I don't really understand. It looks like no one's home though." I point towards the building, emphasizing how dark and empty it looked. Almost haunting.

"That's why it's good to have a friend like me because I can get us in. Another exclusive tour just for us."

"So I bumped up to friend status just that quick? Wow, wouldn't be surprised if we became best friends after this."

Laughing softly, he gestures for me to start walking towards the front door so he could follow behind me. Just like at the Tokyo Skytree, there was a security guard waiting for us inside the front doors. He came out to greet us and gave a stern look to Hendi before turning to me and giving a genuine smile. He wasn't Grant from the skytree, but he did look like he could be his older brother. He had crinkles on the side of his eyes to show that he smiled and laughed more than you would guess. His body was muscled and ripped, reminding me of a pro-wrestler turned actor.

"It's so nice to meet you Ariana. I'm Bruce."

Bruce.

He extended his hand toward me and I looked at Hendi, mouth agape and wide-eyed before shaking Bruce's hand. It was gentle but firm, and it felt like he was trying not to hurt me. I'm surprised he already knew my name.

"Bruce! I've heard so much about you!" My voice raised about three octaves as my nerves started to kick in. I felt like I was meeting Hendi's dad or something. That's the look he had in his eyes when he scolded Hendi and the way Hendi's cheeks flushed red at his glare.

Bruce cocked an eyebrow up, surprised that he was mentioned to me at all, and turns his expression to Hendi.

"Shut up," Hendi says in response, "Just let us in old man. Time's ticking."

"Just be lucky I'm even letting this night continue. We've been blowing your phone up all night, hoping you didn't get kidnapped by one of these crazy fans."

So that explains Hendi looking at his phone and putting it back in his pocket on a huff constantly tonight. He was avoiding phone calls from his team. Half of me hoped it was because he wanted to give me all of his attention, but the other part of me knew not to be too naïve. He just wanted to escape his hectic life.

"Not now Bruce. We'll talk later, okay?" Bruce stares at him for a long while, looking as if he's assessing Hendi's mental state, before realizing he is indeed okay, and nodding in acceptance. He opens the door behind him and lets us file in.

"I'll be waiting outside the front door if you need me. And before you say anything, no I will not leave you alone now that I know where you are, but I also will give you your privacy and distance. Enjoy, and again Mrs.Ariana, it was a pleasure."

I do some form of a curtsy because in that moment, it felt like the only right thing to do, and respond with, "The pleasure was mine Mr.Bruce." He gives me a warm smile then closes the glass doors, leaving Hendi and me alone in this nice sized art museum.

This museum reminded me of all the ones I've seen in the movies. The flooring was a maple almost honey looking brown wood, the walls were completely white, so they won't take away or contrast with any art hanging on them. There was minimal seating, but the seating that was offered looked like a minimalist, black coffee table. The ceiling was decorated in huge recess lights, making it seem like a giant bubble wrap design. I felt like I was in Beyonce's *Ape Shit* music video.

"This exceeds my expectations," I twirl around to face Hendrix after taking it all in.

"You haven't even seen the art yet," he laughs, shaking his head at me. "Come on, let's be a snooty, bougie couple and critic some art."

I walk over to him and he offers me his arm. I snake mine into the hole he provides, resting my forearm into the crook of his elbow. All of my dreams were coming true tonight and my brain just can't keep up. We walk in tandem over to the first art piece that catches my eye. Two women are sitting in a rowboat, dressed in their finest dresses with hats to match.

They looked as if they were born into money and decided to take the boat out to the lake to enjoy the scenery together. It was an oil painting and I loved how I couldn't see the faces of the women, but I could feel them smiling and laughing together.

"You like?" Hendi was watching me intently as I imagined the life story of the women in front of me.

"A lot. The painting has so much life even though it doesn't necessarily breathe." He nods in agreement.

"Let me show you one of my favorite art pieces."

On our way to the particular art piece he wanted to show me, we stopped by and critiqued what felt like hundreds of paintings. On the outside, this building didn't seem all that huge, but walking through on the inside felt like I was navigating through a huge maze. Hundreds and hundreds of western art pieces were decorated on the walls.

We stop in front of a beautiful still-life painting made with oil paint. There was a woman holding a baby in the center and around them was a garland of different flowers. There was so much color surrounding them, and it looked as though she was showing off her baby to the world. The only thing is, there wasn't a smile on her face, and her eyes looked sad.

"When I look at his painting, I think of my dad." Hendi's voice breaks into the silence in a soft whisper tone. "I know it's a mother and her child, but art is meant for us to interpret it our own way, right?"

I just nod and rub up and down his arm because I feel what he's about to say is something that's hard for him to talk about.

"When I was 14, my dad took his own life. He always dreamed of being a guitarist, but those dreams were placed on the back burner when I was born. Ozzy's birth caused them to stop completely, and he ended up falling into a deep depression. Music was his life and his ultimate love." I guide us towards the seating nearby so he could be sitting down while he talked about this.

"Don't get me wrong, he loved my brother and I so much, but music had some supernatural effect on him. He said when he played, it's like his sorrows and worries evaporated because the melodies were telling him everything was okay. Having two young kids though caused him to have to work multiple jobs, leaving no time for music. One day while we were at school and my mom was doing God knows what, he ended it."

I lean my head on his shoulder, trying to comfort him like he did me on the bench by the bridge.

"My dad was everything to me and looking at that painting reminds me that he was present, but he wasn't all the way there. He tried to hide his depression from me and Ozzy but me being the oldest, I could always see right through it. My biggest struggle right now, is forgiving him. I know it's been years but it's just so hard…" his voice breaks with that last word and I pull him into a hug. I take his hat off and place it down next to us, then just squeeze him as hard as I can.

He doesn't sob, but I do feel some tears soaking my dress. I rub his back and we sit like this for some time. Soon, he pulls back from me and I see hurt but also a flicker of anger on his face.

"Sorry," he said, "I don't usually cry."

"Maybe you should." I offer and he just looks at me like I said the world was actually triangle and not round.

"Anyway, after that, my mom really went off the deep end. She was barely present to begin with, but she went crazy after my dad left. She started using drugs and leaving the house for days at a time, leaving me to take care of Ozzy on my own. When my dad was here, I had to do that anyway because he was always working and she was never there, but it hurt more at that time because I didn't know if we'd ever have a parent again. When I turned 18, I filed for custody, took my little brother, and got the hell out of there. They gave me custody because I was making some money from the songs my band was releasing and once, I got him out of there, he became an official member and that's all she wrote."

My heartbreaks for the little boys that had to go through this alone. My heartbreaks for his parents and the downward spiral they went through that resulted from things they had to deal with. But most of all, my heartbreaks for the man in front of me because he is holding all of this hurt and anger inside, afraid to let it out and release it to the world.

"Whatever happened to your mom?" I whisper into his shoulder after I lay back down.

He scoffs at my question, obviously still disgusted with the idea of her.

"She's reached out a couple times when I was 19 begging for some money to help her turn her life around. At that time, our band had a huge fan base and we had just signed with our label. I told her I'd help her by sending her to rehab, but she insisted the money was better.

At that point, I knew she wasn't trying to change and still didn't care about us, so I cut off all communication. Threatened to get her locked up if she called me again. She wasn't helping my mental health and it was hurting me seeing my brother hurt from this. So, I don't know where she is right now."

I nod, understanding his decision and happy that I can put a face – or faces – to the pain.

"I'm sorry that you had to go through all of that so young." I wish I had something better than that to offer him but I'm honestly at a loss for words.

"You don't have to apologize. I'll be okay…eventually. My biggest fear is that I just don't want to end up like … him. Because every day is a struggle for me but I'm working on it, trust me."

"Maybe it's time to seek help from an outside source. Trust *me* when I say it helps to talk someone."

He nods his head but doesn't say anything and I smile at that because to me it feels like a breakthrough. Before I think better of it, I reach up and kiss his cheek. I swear his cheeks glow red for a brief second.

"Thank you for sharing that with me, I know it wasn't easy." I decide to share a little more information with him because I realize we are more alike than different.

"That Beethoven song we played earlier was Grampy's favorite song. He always played it on his piano, and I taught myself how to play it to surprise him for his birthday one year. Ever since then it became our song, and my last time playing it before tonight, was at his funeral."

It felt like we were in a church confessing to all of the things we've done in the past. It was liberating giving that hurt attention and working towards accepting it.

"Are you happy with your career and the music you put out?" I ask on a whim, hoping my gut tells me I'm right. Even though I've only heard one song by him, I feel like it drowned out his true intentions of making it, if that makes sense.

"Not entirely, no." He rubs a hand through his hair. "What makes you ask that?"

"Just a feeling I have."

"Oh, well yea…the answer is no. I mean, I love my songs, but sometimes the label pushes for a more up-tempo, popular sound, so they ask us to speed up the beat to certain songs that I write. I personally feel that with doing that, the message gets lost behind all the crazy 808s and bass. I'm more of a simple man when it comes to delivering a message. I just wish I could execute that how I want. The label doesn't care about what I want though, they only care about making money."

This sounds on brand with what I've been reading about with artists lately and wanting out of their contracts.

"Are you the one that solely makes the decisions for the band, or do the other guys chime in too?"

"I'm the one that started the band, so I make majority of the decisions and they all just go along with it because they love and support my vision. It's the reason they joined the band in the first place. Plus, they just want to play. But I definitely value their opinions and input and allow them to flex their creative wings. I signed the record deal for them. If it was up to me, I wouldn't have signed anything and stayed indie."

I feel as though now I have the complete picture of Hendrix Evans. Troubled past, bad boy but secretly good, nurturing and wants the best for everyone around him. Doesn't take shit if it causes him stress and isn't naïve when it comes to his mother.

Hendi. Music mogul. Will probably reach legend status as time goes on. Stuck and feels trapped, trying to claw his way free. Caring and devoted. Determined.

Perfectly him. Perfectly human, despite what the fans that worship him might think.

We continue sitting there, enjoying one another. He tells me stories from his childhood, and I tell him stories from mine. Good ones to help bring the mood back up. He eventually tells me it's time for our last stop and we head out to the main doors.

Fourteen

"Now for our last destination, we're going to have to take a cab," Hendi says as we exit the building.

"Oh, thank God," I exaggerate my exhaustion by placing my hands on my knees and fake dry heaving, "I feel like we've been walking for days."

"I wish," Hendi says so quietly I almost didn't hear him.

I let it go and chalk it up to him just not wanting to go back to his superstar lifestyle. I feel for him, wishing he could have a normal life again. I can't imagine what it'd be like to have flashing cameras always blinding my view of this beautiful world.

By the way, who knew the world had so many beautiful things to offer?

Hendi showed me more beautiful things in these past few hours than I've ever seen in my whole 22 years of life. He also showed me new experiences and emotions I've never felt before, so I'm having trouble trying to understand them all.

Hendrix grabs my hand and walks over to the end of the street, waving his other hand to hail a taxicab.

I swear it's like he owns this city because not even a full 10 seconds later, a cab with a neon sign on the roof appears out of what seems like thin air and pulls up on the curb beside us. The driver starts to get out to open our doors, but Hendi waves him off and pulls on the handle.

"Your carriage awaits you Madam McNally," he says in a posh British accent, and bows.

"You expect me to place my royal shoes on this concrete filth? Throw your jacket down before I feed you to the wolves." I raise my head up high and cross my arms, tapping my foot.

Hendi laughs but gets right back into character.

"I'm sorry m'lady, I seem to have left my jacket at home."

The taxi driver starts yelling at us and I laugh, finally climbing into the backseat.

It felt like I was in the back of a police car the way the taxi had a privacy glass. I know it was a safety precaution for the driver, but it still felt impersonal. Back home in New Jersey, I always took the train and rarely ever took a cab.

Once we were both in the car and buckled up, Hendi told the driver where we were going in Japanese. The driver peered at me through his rear-view mirror, giving me a small, knowing smile. He then nods at me, and I can't help but smile back.

Where is Hendi taking me?

I look over at him, and he looks down at me, smiles, then grabs and squeezes my hand. I interlock my fingers in his, and lean my head against his shoulder, completely at peace.

This is shaping out to be the best night of my life. Nothing will ever top this.

"LG," Hendi whispers in my ear and I stir out of my sleep. I didn't realize I dozed off and I'm kind of disappointed that I did. I wanted to see the sights and get a hint about where we were going.

I lift my head up from his shoulder and realize that I left a pool of drool in my wake. I quickly wipe my mouth with the back of my hand while he just smiles at me.

"Sorry," I say embarrassingly, turning my face away. The last time I felt this embarrassed was when I started my period for the first time, and my dad was the only one there I had to tell. That was a day, let me tell you.

"For what?" he shrugs off what I did then opens his car door. He rounds the back of the taxi to come and open mine, "Come on."

I reach out and grab the hand he had outstretched towards me and climb out the car.

It's at this moment that I take the time to look at our surroundings. On one side, there were buildings that reminded me of my apartment building. On the other side, however, it's like I was transported to the most beautiful place shown on the travel channel.

There were endless amounts of cherry blossom trees lining a beautiful river stream. The cherry blossoms were all coating the top of the river, so it looked like the river was made of cherry blossoms too.

I feel Hendi interlock his fingers with mine, and he begins to walk towards the bridge that's arching over the river.

"Hendi this is …. beyond gorgeous," I say, surprised I could find my words because upon initially seeing it, I was speechless.

"I think so too. It reminds me of someone I know," he says smirking at me.

We pass couples on the bridge wrapped into each other, some kissing, others taking pictures. We find a free spot on the bridge railing and just peer down at the steady flow of flowers disappearing underneath me.

Hendi pulls me a little closer to him, and I nestle into his side.

"Sometimes, I feel like my life is like a whirlpool. I'm being spun in so many directions, and never have time to calm down and be to myself. Being with you, *tonight*, life felt like this river. Calm, steady, and beautiful. You brought color to a rather dark, gray day. I'll cherish this night for the rest of my life." He taps me on the nose, causing a giggle to fly up my throat.

"I should've known being a singer would make you good with words." I smile up at him.

He gives a nervous chuckle, probably worried about what I'm going to say in response.

"Before Tokyo, my life was like a broken record. Every day was the same, uneventful thing. I didn't think I had a happy ending where I was doing what I loved. But now? Especially after tonight? My life is more like a Rubik's Cube. I never know what turn or move I'm going to make next, but in the end, I know it's going to be unique, full of color and worth it."

He seems to like my reply because he pulls me a little bit tighter next to him, then quickly kisses the top of my head. This display of affection sends a jolt down my spine and a signal straight to the girl below my belly button. She tingles in response, developing an increased heartbeat that mimicked mine.

I've never had such non-sexual intimate moments with a guy, let alone this many in one night.

We watch the flowers dance on top of the river for a few more minutes before something pulls us out of our little world.

"May I have everyone's attention please," a man's voice says from behind us. I turn to see him standing in the middle of the bridge, with a very embarrassed looking woman tucked under his arm. His voice was a little shaky, which tells me he's about to do something nerve wrecking.

I look up at Hendi amused because I think we're about to witness one of the most beautiful things life had to offer.

A proposal.

He seems to be watching the moment intently, genuinely confused and wondering what this screaming guy's problem was.

"Me and my beautiful girlfriend Melissa have been together for 2 years today, and I can't think of any lifetime without her." The man releases the arm he had wrapped around who I'm hoping is Melissa and gets down on one knee.

Her hands fly to her mouth and I can see the tears starting to form in her eyes.

"Melissa, will you do this balding before 30, stress filled man who's still trying to figure out life, the honor of becoming Mrs. Brooks?"

"Yes, yes Ye——-" Her squeals sound a lot like those girls that were chasing after Hendi earlier as she jumps all over her new fiancé.

The whole bridge breaks out into applause and I smile hard, trying to not let my happy tear break free from my eye. I loved beautiful moments like this, which is why it was added in my bucket list. I steal another glance at Hendi who is already looking down at me with a quirked eyebrow.

He claps along but gives me this "wow, that guys bonkers" look.

Once the groom-to-be figures out which finger is the right one through his happy tears, Hendi pulls me away from the crowd and down the street towards the peer like square sitting on top of the water making up the river.

He sits down with one of his legs stretched out in front while the other is bent, with his knee tucked under his arm as he leans on it. Taking off his shades, he rests them in the middle of his V-neck, causing more of his glorious pectorals to peek through.

He pats the space next to him, and I plop down, both feet stretched out in front.

We find a comfortable silence again as we watch the water up close, the sound of the stream singing its beautiful song in my ears. I close my eyes and point my face towards the sky, letting the soft, sweet smelling breeze plant a chaste kiss on my cheek.

"I wish you came in a pocket-sized version," Hendi says a few minutes later, in a low voice from his spot on the small dock.

I smirk as I open one eye and turn my head to look at him. He was staring at me with so much intensity, it made my stomach cramp up. He didn't look like he was joking because his face was hard as stone, almost pained even.

I straighten up from my slouch, and open both eyes, turning my body so I can look at him comfortably.

"I wish I had a little peace with me, everywhere I go. That way, when the road gets tough, and the lifestyle is eating away at my mental sanity, I can pull you out and pull a string on your back that causes that calming voice of yours to tell me everything will be okay. Then I can kiss your forehead every night and breathe in your lemon zest mixed with essential oils scent."

This man right here.

Who gave him the power to fill my heart while breaking it at the same time?

I did. I gave him that power. But we will never work, he even said so himself.

I open and close my mouth multiple times, probably looking like an idiot while I do it. I have no idea what to say to him that won't hurt me but won't send him running for the hills either.

I finally settle on the best word in the English dictionary.

"What?"

"Look, I know I said I don't do monogamy, or long-distance, or anything but one-night stands," I scoff at that last statement because that's exactly what this night is. A one-night stand that *he* initiated and offered.

"But this is different LG. I've never felt this way before about someone, let alone someone I've never even kissed. I'm willing to make this work, and I know this is a long shot, but I want you to come on tour with me. We're on the second leg, so it'll only be a couple months of travel, I can pay for—"

I put my hand up to stop the desperate noises from coming out of his mouth. He sounded nothing like the Hendi I met earlier tonight. He sounded like a little boy begging for his mom to not leave him in his new pre-school class.

"Hendi, I want more than anything to make you and I work but…it just won't. Like you said earlier, distance causes distance. And besides, who's to say you'll even want me in the morning. For all we know, this night could be a fluke and the result of some really good sake."

I offer him an awkward, lop-sided smile to hide the hurt I feel. His jaw ticks and he looks like he's trying to contain his anger. Why is he mad? He's the one who said it wouldn't work first.

"Hendrix—"

His hand grasps the back of my neck, and he crashes his lips onto mine, our teeth hitting each other on the impact. Ignoring it, Hendi's firm, and strong lips work my mouth as his tongue peeks out and licks along my lower lip.

Groaning, I open my mouth to him, and as I do this, his tongue darts in finding mine, forcing it to dance with his. Our kiss grows deeper, hungrier, and he shifts himself so that he's hovering over the top half of my body. I arch my back as I lower down to lay on the small dock, his other hand now getting familiar with the curves I had hiding under this black dress.

He growls into my mouth as I take his lower lip into my mouth, sucking on it hard before biting down a little, drawing a small amount of blood. The metallic, silvery taste mixed with the natural taste of Hendi was enough to leave me drunk for days. I *needed* more of him.

He starts kneading my breasts through my dress at the same time I find his imprint through his pants and squeeze.

Giggles fill the air somewhere behind us and that's when my brain decides to take control of my body again. I guess the same thing goes for Hendi because our kiss becomes more slowed before he eventually (and reluctantly) pulls away. He places his forehead against mine and just rubs up and down the back of my neck with his hand.

We breathe in each other's carbon dioxide for a few moments before separating from each other. I turn behind me to see a group of young kids watching us from behind a car that was parked a few feet away.

Red flushes my cheeks and Hendi gives a small, sad laugh.

"Is that your first time going to second-base?" He asks once he realizes how embarrassed how I am.

"In public, yes," I retort, feeling like a little kid.

"Wow, your last boyfriend was a wanker," he jokes.

I raise an amused eyebrow at him, "What are we British now?"

"We could be if you want. Remember, we control our own narrative LG. If only it were that easy…"

It didn't take much for the mood to quickly shift back to a sad, depressive state.

The silence around us is broken by the sound of my phone ringing. I completely forgot life was still going on outside of our little bubble.

I dig my phone out of my purse and look at who could be calling me at 3:00 am. Of course, it was Theo.

"Hey T," I say, love coating my throat. From the noise I could hear in the background, I'm assuming he's out partying with his coworkers again.

"Arrriana," he slurs my name, "How's it goin'? I just realized I didn't even call to see if you made it home. This is it. This is that call."

I laugh as I visualize how he must look right now. I can imagine him being held up by Jason, his work best friend.

Even though it's entirely too late for him to check on me, I still appreciate the sentiment.

"I'm fine Theo, go back to your party. Talk to you soon. Be safe okay?"

"Whatever you say Ari. Love you." He hangs the phone up and I tuck mine back in my purse, smiling at my idiot friend.

"Boyfriend?" I hear Hendi asking as he sits close to me.

When did he get this close?

"Best friend," I correct him, "I told you I was single as hell."

He nods then turns his attention back to the cherry blossoms. I give an involuntary shiver and rub my arms to keep myself warm.

He glances at me then lets out a sigh. "I guess I can't keep you to myself forever, huh? Time to start the farewell tour."

Standing up, he turns to me and offers his hand. I grab it and he pulls me up in one swift motion, causing me to fall into his chest and our faces to be less than 10 cm away.

I clear my throat, straightening myself and taking a step back.

"Let's walk to the street and I'll call a cab," his eyes are glossing over, and I can tell he's putting on his fake, performer face on, the one that he said he uses when he handles press things and has to put on a mask for the cameras.

It hurts my heart to see that he feels he needs to be fake with me, but this is where our story ends and we both have to find ways to move on with life like nothing happened.

We start our walk up the stairs and towards the road, finding a comfortable stride. Hendi pulls his hat down lower, places his sunglasses on his face, then tucks his hands in his pockets.

When we get to the street, he stops walking and turns to me.

"I think I'm in love with you."

My head goes reeling and I feel like the ground beneath me is spinning. Did he just say what I think he said? I open my mouth to protest, to tell him he's just high on the moment and the prospect of wanting to be in love, but his forefinger pushes up against my lips to keep me from talking.

"I know it sounds crazy, and I don't care if the feeling isn't mutual. I always trust my heart rather than my mind, and my heart never lies to me. He was the one, in fact, to tell me to take a chance on you." He releases his finger and walks off in front of me, leaving me to stand in my own puddle of confusion.

I run to catch up and reiterate why this will never work, but he just shakes his head as soon as I match his pace.

"Don't say it, I know." Is all he offers me before we're in silence again.

He waves for a cab and just like earlier, one pops up out of thin air like he was Lord of the cabs or something.

He reaches to open my door, not looking at me, and I move to stand in front of him, blocking the door from fully opening.

"Hendi, we need to talk about thi—"

"When we meet again, you will be mine." He says simply, and it pisses me off.

Why does he think he gets the final say in my life?

"Who says we'll meet again," I scoff at him and he gives me his megawatt, brighter than a thousand suns smile, that causes my mouth to glue shut and my ears to open.

"My heart never lies. See you around Ariana," he pulls the cab door open further as I step to the side. I stand there staring at him for a long minute, drinking in his features so I'll never forget him. I want to take a picture so I can know this night was real, and not just one big lucid dream.

I wanted a pocket-sized Hendrix.

He tries his best not to point his face towards me, but I can feel his eyes digging into me behind his shades.

I climb into the back of the cab before I do something I'll regret, like drop my whole life for a man I just met outside a flower shop.

He closes the door behind me, then rounds the front of the cab to give the driver directions on where to take me. Once he's done, he walks back to the curb, then taps the hood of the cab.

I pull out my phone to put my address into the GPS to make sure the driver goes the right way, before looking back up to stare at Hendi as I ride off into the lonely, suffocating night.

When I looked up though, he was gone.

It's like he was just a figment of my imagination. Like he was never there to begin with. That can't be true though, because I can feel his warmth all over me, and smell his manly shampoo and after-shave on my top lip.

When we meet again, you will be mine.

I shake my head, sadness washing over me, and I slouch far down into the cabs back cushion. Closing my eyes, I try to forget Hendi and everything he made me feel, but I can't.

Well Ari, looks like falling for someone in one night wasn't just something that happened in the movies.

The only difference was, I didn't get my happily ever after. I didn't get the prince. All I got was a tease. The sampler.

When we meet again.

"When we meet again," I whisper to the window. Hoping my message travels to its intended receiver.

Fifteen

Hendrix

One year later

Tours.

I fucking hate them.

Always on the road, never have enough time to even get familiar with a roll of tissue before you're off to another venue, in another town, city, and country.

I'm glad this is the last show because after this, I'm not doing another tour for a long time. I'm quitting my label, going indie, and becoming the artist that I want to be.

My fans don't like it? Fuck it, they weren't real fans to begin with, were they?

I was tired of dragging myself around, playing Pinocchio to a room full of Geppettos in suits. I was done having my life placed in the hands of those who could give two shits about me.

I was done.

I was also done giving the people around me who I call family, shit. They didn't deserve to be punching bags to my sorry, heartbroken, and depressed cocoon. It was time to pick my head out my ass and accept the fact that my heart will be missing a piece for a while.

I will be missing a piece of myself until that piece finds her sweet, innocent looking ass back home where she belongs.

With me.

My last show was in New Jersey, which is ironically, the same place LG said she was from. I wonder if she googled me after that night. I wondered if she picked up on the new songs I started performing on the tour.

All those new songs were about her. They were an open letter to her. An open letter to myself. It was also a challenge to see if she'd ever show her face and take responsibility for completely stealing my heart away.

My little grasshopper.

You just had to hop in my life at the worst possible time, then hop away and take everything with you, leaving me with just an empty shell and somewhat of a brain. Somewhat.

Loud banging on the outside of my dressing room door pulls me from my thoughts and reminds me that the show must go on.

"Hey H," my little brother, Ozzy, pokes his head through the door. "They're ready for us now, so get your sorry ass up so we can kill this show."

I give a loud, feral groan as I push out of my chair, grabbing my electric guitar, Chérie, from where she sat in her stand.

"Just give me one more night girl," I kiss her neck and follow Ozzy out into the commotion.

The sound of the crowd cheering and screaming grows louder as we approach the stage. I dap up Ritchie, our drummer, and Kyle, our bassist.

Our hype man, J-Rock --- Jason if he's in front of his grandparents --- introduces each band mate. When their names are called, Ritchie and Kyle make their way to their designated instruments. The crowd goes crazy and they both wave, giving humble nods before nodding at each other.

Ozzy's name is called next and the crowd erupts even louder as he takes a seat at his keyboard.

I'm last to walk out, and as I do, the crowd goes ballistic. I thought when Ozzy went on, it was impossible for them to get louder. I couldn't be more wrong. I take my place in front of the mic and raise Cherie up in the air.

"Let's do this," I say calmly before bringing Cherie down, and brushing my guitar pick on her strings, causing a loud melody of sounds to erupt from the amps splayed out in front.

Even though I can't see the crowd due to the blinding lights on stage, I can still feel their energy, and it's what keeps me coming onto this stage every night. It's what caused me to settle with being Pinocchio.

But I found something new to give me energy, and this just won't cut it for me anymore.

We start our set, and I start singing old songs from our older albums.

As the night goes on, and our songs start to slow down, we've reached the point in the show where I decided to add in some of the new songs I wrote.

Some of her songs.

The band leaves me on the stage alone as I perform these next 30 minutes. They'll be back to close out the show, and possibly perform an encore.

As I start to sing the words to the first song, I get lost in them, and memories of that night in Tokyo start to flood back. I close my eyes and let my fingers do the work as Cherie and I sing a sorrowful duet about loss, heartbreak and wanting peace in this chaotic world.

On the chorus, something causes me to open my eyes, and when I do, they lock onto a sea of light brown.

My mind wants to freeze up and stop all movement in my body, but my heart tells me to keep playing, so I do.

I play for me, and I play for her.

And then I sing to her, letting every emotion I feel drip into my voice and lace the microphones wire, causing the message to flow to the speakers so she can feel it.

Really feel it.

Me and you are night and day

You bring the color to my dark and brooding face

As fast as you rose, you went and set

And my blissful piece of sun came and left

If we ever meet, you will be mine

You need to pay for this unforgiven crime

I played and played, one song after the other, until I ended up playing all of the songs I wrote about her. I couldn't read the emotion in her eyes, but I sure as hell felt all the emotion pouring out of mine.

Everyone around her erupted into cheers, whoops, and hollers, but our gazes remained fixed on each other. It was then that I noticed she was wearing our tour merch and I smirked at her. She looked down, then back up, letting a smile spread across her flawless face.

God, she was perfect. And she was going to be mine.

We finished up the show, and as soon as the last song was done, I ran backstage to tell the bodyguards to bring her back here. I couldn't waste any more time.

If it was just me on that stage, I would've ended the show a long time ago and ran off with her into the sunset. But it wasn't just me and I had other people to think about, like Ozzy.

Bruce, my main bodyguard, gave me a "really?" look, thinking it was one of my one-night stand situations.

"Just do it," I sigh patting him on the shoulder, "You can give me that dad lecture later."

He shakes his head at me, then makes his way to the crowd. I'm nervous as shit and try to fix my hair so I can look presentable and not exhausted from all of that performing.

My band mates smack me on the back and invite me to take shots with them on the tour bus, but I told them to go ahead without me. Ozzy gave me a once over before deciding I was, in-fact, still his older brother and not a complete stranger, before following after the other guys.

A few rapid heartbeats and pep-talking's later, I see Bruce approaching me at the corner of my eye.

When I turn to face him, I'm stopped dead in my tracks at the sight of Ariana.

I've thought this moment over and over in my head since the night we departed, but none of that could ever prepare me for this.

For this emotion, for the drop-dead gorgeous beauty in front of me, or the flashing ring I saw strangling her wedding finger.

She was married.

I just stare at the ring, and I see that she glances down to see what I'm staring at. She laughs when she realizes what it is and takes a step towards me.

"Hendi, it's so good to see you," her beautiful, calming, torturous voice fills my ears. I dreamt of that voice every night.

F…uck, shes married!?

My jaw twitches as I tense and try to keep my cool.

"You're married." I state, looking at the ring again. I spent all this time waiting for us to come back to each other, and she went and shit all over my fucking parade.

It's probably her best friend, that prick. I could tell he loved her by the sound of his voice on her phone that night.

She looks down at the ring, then back up at me, irritated. *She's* irritated with *me?* Wow.

She pulls the ring off, then hands it to the person I just realized was standing next to us. She was an older looking woman, probably in her late 20s, wearing a matching merch shirt as LG.

"No, I'm not. This is Ava's ring. She thought it'd be funny to prank you, but I told her you weren't going to fall for it. Guess jokes on me."

I let out the breath I didn't realize I was holding before running my hands through my hair.

"Forgive me if I came off rude, but I *have* been waiting on you to show your face for a year now. I was starting to doubt my heart," I joke, hopefully to get rid of the irritation I caused.

Her face softens again, and she gives me a smirk, similar to the one I gave her a few minutes ago on stage.

"I thought your heart never lies," she retorts.

"That depends," I say as I reach out to grab her hand and pull her into me. I breathe in the smell of her sweat from going crazy at my concert, her sugary, honey smelling shampoo, and her perfume. If I didn't know any better, I'd say she got dolled up just for me.

Good thing I don't know any better.

"Will you be mine LG? The tour is over, and I plan on taking a much-needed break from this life. I even have my own place in New Jersey."

Her eyes go wide at this revelation.

"When did you—"

"Don't get your panties in a bunch. I didn't do it to stalk you or anything. Not a serial killer, remember? I coincidentally already had a place before we met. I never used it though, and ended up renting it out as a B & B."

"Why didn't you ever tell me that?" She pulls back from where I'm holding her tight in my arms, to eye me suspiciously.

"You never asked," I joke, poking her on the nose.

"So whatya say LG? Put this fucker out of his misery and go dutch on this relationship bill?"

She puts her head in my chest and looks as though she's about to give me the worst sting of rejection ever experienced by man.

I'm about to add a few more words to seal the deal before she leans back again, and says, "I only have enough for the tip, so I hope that's okay."

She gives me that same lopsided smile from under the cherry blossom trees, the one that I wanted to kiss away and tell her everything will work out.

Make her believe my heart was the real thing.

"Baby, I'll take anything you're willing to give me," and with that, I sign on the dotted line.

We kiss like no one's around, dry humping each other to oblivion. Bruce clears his throat and I wave him off, but then Ava clears hers and asks Bruce, "Um, could you show me to the bathroom?"

They leave and I continue satisfying that craving that's been itching at the back of my throat all this time.

The craving of sunshine, peace, and laughter.

The craving of strawberry Chapstick, and honeysuckle lips.

The craving of a new life, and new possibilities.

Love, and her.

Fucking her…

Epilogue

Ariana

Two years later

"Seriously Theo, are you okay today? You've missed our exit twice now and I'm starting to think you're taking me to a ditch to murder me. Cold hard murder. Is that what you want on your conscious?"

I cross my arms in the passenger seat and look at Theo. He told me he wanted to go buy clothes to revamp his wardrobe, so I've been dragging behind him all day to do that.

I flew back to Tokyo a couple of days ago because he was begging me to visit, and eventually bought my plane ticket and said, "You're coming and that's it."

I told him I was sick and tired of looking at clothes after being in multiple shops non-stop for over 5 hours.

He told me he'd take me to Nabezo Shinjuku Meiji Dori as a thank you, and of course I can't say no when he bribes me like that. But now, he's *definitely* passed the exit a couple of times, and after living in Tokyo for 10 months before moving back home, I've gotten to know the exit for Nabezo pretty well.

"Relax, I'm just taking a new route. I like our car ride talks," he gives me puppy dog eyes and I roll mine, not buying his act for a second.

"If you're taking me to another clothing store Theodore, I swear on everything I'm catching a cab all the way back to your apartment." I turn my head towards the window to look at my unfamiliar surroundings.

About 15 minutes later, he pulls into a parking lot next to some residential looking buildings. I recognized those buildings. I saw them every weekend while I was in Tokyo since that night. I even took Theo here once I got the courage to tell him about my adventurous night with a superstar. He thought I was drunk when I told him, but when I finally brought Hendi home, he believed me.

"Is this your way of apologizing? Taking me to my favorite spot?"

He doesn't respond, just gets out the car then walks to the back of it. I shake my head and smile at my friend for trying to make up for the blisters in my feet. I had on heels because I was trying to be cute while I was out for a little, but that completely backfired.

I reach down in my purse as my passenger door opens, "I hope you brought snacks cause I'm—"

"Hey beautiful." I stop rummaging in my bag and turn to the familiar voice.

"Ozzy!? What are you doing here?" I jump in his arms and he shakes me around before setting me down. He was Hendi's little brother and ended up becoming like the brother I never had. We got close quick, and I know that made Hendi happy to see the two most important people in his life loving each other.

"Oh, I was just in the neighborhood."

I look around for Theo, but he was nowhere to be seen. What the hell?

Ozzy leads me over to the bridge where I can see figures standing all along the edges. When we get closer, I realize, it's my family.

My dad, my mom, Theo, Bruce, Ritchie, Kyle, Ava, everyone we cherished. What were they all doing here?

I run up to each one of them and give them a hug, happy tears flooding my face because we haven't seen much of each other since I started my new job at this lab in Manhattan.

"We're just here for the show," Kyle offers, and my dad squeezes my hand from behind. I turn to look at him, and he nods down towards the water.

That's when I notice little floating lotus lights drifting down the river with small candles lit inside of them. I followed the trail of the flowers until I saw where they originated from at the small dock. Hendi was there, standing with a suit on, hopping from foot to foot, adjusting his pants nervously.

My boyfriend, the man of my dreams, was standing in the exact spot we shared our first kiss. I ran from where I was on the bridge down to the dock toward Hendrix.

When he heard me approaching, he quickly straightened up and was standing in the middle of the dock, cherry blossoms covered the dock floor, with lotus flowers lining the side.

He gave a broad, nervous looking smile as I descended the stairs and stopped in front of him at the dock.

"Hey love," he sang as he leaned down to kiss me.

"Hendi, what is all this? What are you doing here?" I kiss him as his lips touch mine, slow and passionate, forgetting that my father was standing by, witnessing it all.

Hendi pulls away from me and wraps his arm around my neck, tucking me under his armpit.

"May I have everyone's attention please," he yells toward the bridge, but everyone was already intently staring at us. "Me and my beautiful girlfriend Ariana have been together for 2 years today, and I can't think of any lifetime without her."

I'm confused at first, but then I remember the proposal on the bridge almost two years ago, and swat him in his rib for making fun of them.

Wait. Was this my dream proposal? Can't be, Hendi said he wasn't a fan of marriage right now. Not like I was either, but still…

"I'm kidding, I'm kidding," He says as he releases me then turns to face me. He grabs both of my hands in each of his and stares intently in my eyes.

"Ari, when I first saw you, I knew you were different. You woke up a curiosity in me that I longed for years to find. You made this walking skeleton more than just a pile of bones. You gave me flesh, then skin, then caused my heart to beat which brought warmth through my veins.

My heart was yours to take from the moment I saw you bending down to sniff those flowers. The moment you let me hide behind your bush. The moment you gave me those eyes that said I was an idiot and sexy all at the same time." He winks at me and I let the waterfall of tears roll down my face

"The moment I watched you run down the street helpless was the moment my heart was *yours* to take."

He shakes his head at my interruption before continuing.

"Last time we were here together, it was a tragic end to a beautiful night. But now? It will be our new colorful beginning. Beginning of forever. Will you do this balding before 30, stress filled man—"

I crash my lips to his, cutting off his second round of mocking. Everyone on the bridge doesn't know if they should cheer yet, so I stop the kiss and squeal like Melissa did.

"Yes, yes a thousand times yes!" I say as I resume the kiss. Cheers erupt, and everyone runs down to congratulate us.

I can't believe this.

I won.

I got my happily ever after.

I got the prince.

Looks like he wasn't the sampler, but the full, three course meal.

And he was mine.

All mine.

When in Tokyo

Enjoyed reading *When in Tokyo*? How about checking out my *Cloudy Day* series which follows the story of Jordan Jameson and Malakai Woods. The final installment of this book series will be coming out late 2021.

On A Cloudy Day (Cloudy Day #1)

Clear Skies (Cloudy Day #2) – Coming Soon

Not ready to dive into Jordan and Malakai's story yet? Check out these standalones also by me.

Lunar Thoughts: A Poetry Book

When in Tokyo

Stay up to date on future books by following me on all social media platforms @Manitheauthor , or visiting my website http://manitheauthor.com . Subscribe to the newsletter and be one of the first notified on everything Imani.

Acknowledgements

First and foremost, I'd like to shout out my co-author, Ms. Emery Sumter. I had no idea I was pregnant with her when I started writing this story, but I'd like to give all the creative credit to her. Without her knowledge, she gave me the will power to keep going. My beautiful, smart, happy baby. Mommy loves you to the moon and beyond.

I want to say thank you to all of you reading and who continue to support me on this crazy journey. I have been writing since I was a kid and the fact that I'm able to entertain and give you guys the same feelings I get when I read is so surreal. I can never say thank you enough.

I want to give an enormous thanks to Kerry, the mastermind behind the cover design. I told her my vision and she was the only person I could find who was able to execute it exactly how I pictured in my head. Thank you for letting me pop your book cover cherry, Kerry. (I'm lame, I know).

To my family for their never-ending support. I hope you know how much I appreciate you all. I love you love you love you.

Can't wait to see everyone in the next book!
Until then, all my love.

About Imani

Imani is a new graduate and mother, graduating with a bachelor's degree in marketing just one month after giving birth to her first child. She is an amazon bestselling author, thanks to her debut novel *On A Cloudy Day*.

Not only is she an author, but she is a singer/songwriter, poet, and plays multiple instruments. You can listen to her debut EP *Night Owl* anywhere you stream your music.

She loves koalas, fried food, and deformed/misshapen stuffed animals (She finds beauty in the broken you could say lol).

176

Check out this preview of my book *On A Cloudy Day*,
the first installment to the *Cloudy Day* series.

PROLOGUE

Lifted.

Floating.

Ascending towards the sky.

I feel almost weightless as my body glides upwards. I look around me to try and figure out where I am but there's nothing. Darkness and what appear to be stars is all I see around me.

I try to reach my hand out to touch one, but I can't move. I look towards the force that's pulling me up, and I'm met with nothing but a bright light. It's like I'm being pulled into the sun, but the heat is subtle, and I can barely feel it.

My arms and legs are dangling at my sides, making my body form an upside-down U. My hair is flowing around my face as if it's in space defying gravity.

As I get closer to the star, I must squint to keep from going temporarily blind, but it doesn't help as I'm pulled into the stars embrace like a warm gentle hug. I close my eyes, succumbing to the feeling pulsating through me, like a crackling of energy zapping through my veins. I hear the star softly whisper my name, caressing my ear drums with its soft voice.

Jordan, it says once.

Jordan.

It sounds like it's coming from everywhere and nowhere at the same time.

Jordan! it says more harshly, and I snap my eyes open as the star I'm floating in starts to shake.

Pieces of its barrier begin to break off like puzzles, giving me a peak of the starry abyss I traveled through to get here. Panic starts to flicker in my lower stomach as I watch the gentle euphoria I bathed in, dim its light and come crashing down.

JORDAN

"JORDAN!" I shoot out of my sleep and collide my head with something hard and huge. "Ow! What the hell !?" I hear someone say in the fuzzy space beside me.

I rub my forehead, then eyes, as I try to gain consciousness and clear the sleep out of my eyes. Focusing on my surroundings, I see that I'm in my childhood bedroom. I take in my Tame Impala poster over my desk next to the dry erase board emphasizing the importance of today's date.

MOVE IN DAY.

"Really Jordan? I wake you up early like you asked, and you thank me by trying to crack my skull open?"

I look to my right and see Rylie lying on the floor massaging the spot where my forehead collided with hers. I try to stifle my laughter while looking at my best friend, but it overtakes me and I plop back on my bed, almost coughing up a lung. I peak over at her and notice her frown was replaced with a smile and she starts laughing too.

"I see you managed to successfully wake the hibernating bear," I hear my stepdad Benny, short for Benjamin, call on the other side of the door. I roll my eyes gently as my laughter starts to die down.

Don't get me wrong, I love Benny, but sometimes I think he forgets that I'm 20 and not 2. Or maybe, he's trying to make up for the time he wasn't in my life from the ages of newborn to 10. Either way, his intentions are pure, so I let it slide and humor him sometimes.

I pull the covers up over my head trying to see if I can disappear back into my peaceful slumber by shutting reality out.

"Don't make me bring Ben in here to sing his wake-up song to you," Rylie says to my right. I guess my experiment didn't work.

I groan loudly and finally raise back up and eventually out of my bed. I stretch as I watch Ry grab a few unfolded boxes from my closet. "Hurry up and get your moving clothes and attitude together, we need to beat this move in day traffic."

"Why are you so gung-ho about moving? Last week you almost cried about having to leave your hamster for another year," I snort as I make my way to the same closet she pulled boxes from to find my go-to chill outfit.

"Well, last week Theodore didn't shit in my hand as I tried to tell him I loved him. Besides, my mom started getting on my nerves about the whole 'hurry up and secure an internship' fiasco and I am in desperate need of release from her overbearing grasps."

I change into some Nike workout leggings and a cream-colored oversized hoodie that had the initials CAU on the front. Slipping my feet into some white, black and red Air Max 95s, I grab the last of the boxes from the closet and toss them into the pile Rylie created in the middle of my room.

"You know your mom just wants the best for you. She's trying to make sure you're set in life," I shrug as I move towards my desk and start to pack up my essentials. She groans, "why do you sound just like her?"

"We might've had a few secret meetings behind your back," I say playfully winking at her, "Now start packing. I know you didn't wake me up just to watch."

"Ah, my plan is foiled." We both laugh and start to work on packing up my room.

About 3 hours later, we finish putting everything I need into boxes and head downstairs. I see my mom working on breakfast for all of us in the beautiful open spaced kitchen.

Our kitchen is something you'd see on HGTV and is used as inspiration when you want to renovate your house. We have a huge island in the middle with white quartz countertops and cream-colored cabinets. Along the front side of the island we had 4 barstools and placemats we only set out as decoration. Our dishwasher was next to our stove and blended in with the cabinets, so you couldn't even tell it was a dishwasher. Our refrigerator was the same way and had so much space, you could fit two dead bodies in there. You know, if you wanted to at least.

My mom was at the stove flipping pancakes and adding them to the leaning tower of cakes on the plate to the right of her. Benny oversaw the fruit cutting for our homemade fruit cups. I think he chooses this job just so he can slip and eat some of the fruit as he cuts. I wouldn't even put it past him if that was the case. I also know that he sneaks my little brother, Jamie, some grapes to keep him sedated and from jumping all over the counters. He was only two, but this little boy was a firecracker. He was also the love of my life and takes up all the space in my heart currently. Not like anyone else would ever be able to anyway.

"Morning Mom," I say as I kiss her cheek. She smiles and scrunches up her nose in response. My mom was so cute with her little antics and sweet spirit. It hurts me whenever I see her hurting or in pain, both physically and emotionally.

"Morning my Jor. Morning to you too Ryles," she says air kissing towards Rylie and quickly turning back to the pancake tower to concentrate as she tries to add another pancake to the top.

I saunter over to Jamie and play peek-a-boo with him behind Benny's back. He was sitting on the counter next to Ben, with his little feet hanging off the side of the island. He laughs a hearty laugh that melts my insides even more than he already did.

"Morning Buu," I say as I stop playing peek-a-boo and walk up to poke his belly.

He got the nickname Buu because when he was a baby, he was so chubby with a lot of rolls that he reminded me of a milk chocolate colored Majin Buu.

"Jo-Jor! Jo-Jor!" I smile at his nickname for me and kiss his forehead. "Yuckie!" he says as he tries to wipe my kiss off.

"Uh-uh Buu, my love is forever. Sorry," I poke his nose then go take a seat on one of the barstools.

Rylie has already made herself comfortable on her unassigned-assigned barstool seat that's been "hers" since she and I have been friends.

That's about 18 years.

Now, she's munching on some bacon from the bacon platter my mom laid out on the island, next to the scrambled egg platter and syrup cup.

"Okay girls, after breakfast we're heading straight to the school. Move in starts at 8, so we only have 30 minutes to get it movin'," Ben says this as he gyrates his hips and I cringe so hard it hurts.

"Uncle Ben please stop," Ry says as she puts her head into her hands from secondhand embarrassment.

Once they finish preparing breakfast, we all move to the dining table in the dining room to the left of the kitchen. We eat as we talk about the long day we have ahead of us. My mom jokes about Jamie being old enough to help carry the boxes up to my dorm, and Benny countered by saying Jamie could drive the car there and do all the work while we go to the movies.

After Rylie finishes her third helping, we decide to just drag her away from the food because we were going to be late. She snuck a couple more pieces of bacon and reluctantly followed behind us. We got to the school and sure enough, it was packed.

This was my third year in college, and I attended Clark Atlanta University. It was one of the big three alongside Spelman and Morehouse. My mom was a Spelman Alumni and when I told her which college I chose; she was excited for me to experience the culture. My stepdad Ben, however, was from Florida, so he went to the University of Miami and still wasn't used to the downtown Atlanta college life.

As we arrive to the school, we see police officers directing traffic and a whole bunch of golf carts that the housing employees use to get around during this hectic time. First order of business was to figure out which room me and Rylie would be in this year.

We packed up her room a couple of days ago and already loaded it into my mom's Audi SUV. She stayed the night at my place the rest of the time. We roomed together the past couple of years and stayed in a traditionally styled dorm room. It was a great experience, but we both needed more space, so we applied for an apartment style this year. We applied last year too, but they gave them all to the upperclassmen.

I was driving my mom's car and my mom, Benny, and Jamie were in Ben's car following behind me. I finally pull into the housing office parking lot after waiting in a little traffic from all the families in attendance and new freshman.

"Maybe I'll finally find a man this year, cross fingers," Rylie says as she looks out the window at the new students she doesn't recognize. I shake my head at her, "You don't need a man when you have me," I chuckle as I put the car in park towards the back of the lot.

"Last time I checked, you couldn't make the inside of my thighs quiver, and If you could, I would've been elevated this relationship years ago."

"I could easily do that with a little help from some toy- "

"OKAY! This conversation is over," Rylie sing-songs while opening her car door and hopping out.

"Alright Jo-bear, Ry-Tie, you ready to get this show on the road?" Ben walks from his parking spot a couple cars away and meets us at mom's Audi.

"Uncle Ben, we're on school grounds, I am now a stranger to you," Rylie says as she puts on her shades. Ben laughs and starts walking towards the housing building. He notices my curious look as I search behind him for my mom and Jamie.

"Jamie fell asleep and your mom didn't want to wake him because he, quote 'looks too adorable right now' unquote, so she'll join us for the fun part." I'm not at all disappointed by this because I knew

Jamie would become agitated from standing still in a line for too long and would want to explore. He's just like me in that aspect, wanting to dabble in any and everything that seems interesting; ready to discover a world anew. Let's just hope he isn't *fully* like me and has an idea of what he wants to do with his life.

"Uncle Ben, nobody verbally says quote like that anymore," Rylie says shaking her head and laughing. As we enter the housing line, Ben cocks his head at her seeming genuinely confused and says, "I'm sorry stranger, do I know you?"

"Ha Ha," she retorts sarcastically and lightly punches his arm. We move forward in line and we're almost to the front desk.

"I hope they gave us the apartment style we requested," I turn my head toward Ry.

"If they don't want a call from an angry black woman they better had," she scrunches her eyebrows together trying to look intimidating.

I gasp suddenly. "What if we have suite style? How would we fit your inflated ego?" I place my hand over my mouth. After a beat, I bust out laughing and she rolls her eyes.

"I don't have time for you guys today. I don't want to embarrass myself in front of my unknown future husband."

We get to the desk and find out we got granted the last available apartment unit and we almost scream from excitement. We get the keys and they tell us the move-in instructions, but I'm too busy planning out the many ways I'm going to rearrange my room this school year.

Back at Bens Audi coupe (yea this family lives for the Audi brand), we meet up with my Mom and relay the information to her. Next thing I know, we're at the Heritage Building unloading the truck into our apartment. We're on the second floor so it's not that bad of a move.

Some of the housing employees help us move in, and I learned from the disaster that was move in day last year, that the earlier you are, the more people that are here to help and the faster the job gets done. This is because everyone is pumped up on adrenaline, and the caffeine they consumed that morning in preparation for today.

Two guys named Zavier and Jodie help us move in, and I can tell Rylie already has her eyes set on at least one of them. I, on the other hand, am trying to get my hands on the nearest home goods so I can decorate our living space and cover up the ugliness of the pre-given furniture in the apartment. Jamie is in our living area playing his educational games on his iPad, while my mom unpacks me and Rylie's boxes and takes them to our respective rooms.

Before I know it, we've unpacked everything and took a trip to Home Goods, Target, Hobby Lobby and Walmart.

"Wow, we did a good job," My Mom says as she places both hands on her hip and glances around.

"Goo-Job!" Jamie says as he jumps up excited trying to give me a high five.

"Yes Buu, Good Job," I say high fiving him.

"Well I'm pooped," Rylie says plopping down on the couch in the living area.

"Want to go out to eat to celebrate?" Ben asks us after placing the last Gatorade we bought in the fridge.

"No thanks Uncle Ben, we're going to order some pizza like last year. You know, tradition and all that good stuff," Rylie says waving her hand in the air.

"Pizza! Pizza!" Jamie says as his eyes almost bulge out of his sockets.

"Welp, looks like we have to order pizza tonight now too," my mom chuckles as she looks at Jamie with adoration in her eyes. I look around the room and smile at my unconventional family. Rylie's parents are a part of that family too, but they had to go to a wedding in New York and couldn't make it to the move in day. Rylie was excited to find that out because she did not want her mom in here questioning everyone about on campus job opportunities, the curfew policy, and asking students if they needed an extra study buddy.

Rylie's mom was a lot to handle, which is why I'm surprised her and my mom became best friends in the first place. My mom is the calm serene breeze and Rylie's mom is the storm that comes to blow your house into a dimension with little singing dwarfs. Her Dad is like my mom, chill and laid back, but he also is hilarious and knows how to have fun. Oh, and he's a sucker when it comes to his "little girl Ry Ry". Rylie claims she's annoyed by this nickname, but I know deep down she loves it.

My other best friend, Camille, and her grandmother were also missing. This was because Camille always worked nonstop and barely even had time for herself.

"Okay girls, we'll leave you to it. Come give me a hug," my mom says smiling with her eyes gleaming and I can already see the tears forming.

Me and Ry give my mom a hug and as she hugs us, she says, "I am so proud of you guys, and I know you're destined to do great things, so I am never worried about you. Though I am worried about the actual journey you'll take and the ups and downs I can't prevent. Just never forget to breathe okay?" I feel the tears from her eyes start to run down the side of my face and I pull back to look at her.

"I love you mom."

I wasn't a crier, in fact, I felt like crying didn't do anything but make me look weak and affected. I rarely cried in public or even private.

I hear Rylie trying to suppress a sob, so I pull her away from my mom and try to get her to gather herself. "Okay, I'll call your mom when I get in the car Rylie, to let her know how the move in day went. Make sure you text her too because you know how worrisome she can be."

"I know Auntie, I will. I love you too," Ry says wiping her eyes.

"Alright love bugs bring it in," Ben says as he gathers everyone into another hug. "You get in here too booger!" he says too a trouble making Jamie, already trying to get into some cabinets.

Jamie runs over and crashes into my leg and I laugh as we're all connected in a big group hug. After a few seconds we reluctantly let go and my family leaves.

"Then there was two," I say as I turn from the closed front door of our apartment, "Please tell me you already started up your Papa John's app. I'm in need of some greasy fattening food right now."

"One Alfredo Spinach for you and one Buffalo Chicken for me," Rylie says towards me, but her face is looking down at her phone screen. I can't hide the huge smile on my face as I think about the amazingness I'm about to gobble down in about 50 minutes.

"Have I ever told you I loved you?" I ask her, plotting down on the couch next to her.

"Only like a gazillion times, but it doesn't hurt to say it one more," she winks at me.

For the next couple hours, we eat our pizza while binge watching The Office for the 100th time because how can you ever get tired of The Office?

I look over at the clock and notice it's 2:00am and turn to a snoring Rylie. She's sprawled out, with the blanket hanging off the lower half of her body. She's laying on the couch next to the accent chair I moved too when the pizza arrived.

I turn off the TV and pull her blanket up to cover her whole body, then throw away all the trash we have on the coffee table. I put our leftovers in the fridge then go to my room so I can crash.

As I snuggle into my bed, I give a relaxed sigh and silent prayer that this school year flies by smoothly as I slowly ease into that peaceful abyss that is sleep.

MALAKAI

Still.

Motionless.

Quiet.

I raise my head from my hands as I take in my surroundings.

It's a blanket of white cushion looking fluff. It's almost like I'm sitting on a cloud.

It's so warm here.

I look to where I'm sitting and notice I'm on a stone bench, kind of like one you would see in the Hercules or the 300 movie. I'm wearing the clothes I must've fell asleep in and my skin is glowing just a bit, like it's concealing some type of cosmic energy.

Where am I?

I look around more and notice that the white cotton candy looking fluff goes on forever like it has no end. Didn't I have this dream before? Yes. I've had a similar dream, but I wasn't sitting on a bench in them with my arms resting on my knees, and it didn't start off with my head in my hands.

In the other dream I was in this cloud looking world, but I was walking like I knew where I was going. Like I had a set destination. Is there anyone else here? Should I try to call out? Why can't I stand up? Why can I only move my arms?

I start to panic but that quickly fades when I notice a small glowing blip in the distance ahead of me. It seems to be growing bigger. What is that?

As it grows larger and larger, I realize that it's floating closer to me. It sort of resembles that glowing bubble Glinda in the Wizard of Oz floated down in to meet Dorothy.

How am I still thinking of movie references in my dreams? And why is this blip getting closer? It's starting to get hot in here. I should shade my eyes. I place my arm over my eyes when the blip comes to a stop. I'm squinting because the light is so bright, it's like I'm looking directly at the sun.

Malakai.

Did it just say my name?

Malakai.

Okay clearly, I'm going crazy.

It calls my name again, but in a slow mesmerizing way that has me lowering my arm and staring at it in awe. I feel as though I'm in a trance. I reach my arm out to touch it, curiosity getting the best of me. I don't even know why I'm trying to touch it. You can't touch light, let alone a star, and this blip had to be a star with the way it was blinding me. But still, my arm moved towards it.

Mesmerized.

Malakai.

Closer.

Mesmerized.

Malakai.

Almost there.

When my fingers brush the light, it bursts, and consumes me.

Beep-Beep. Beep-Beep. Beep-Beep. My fingers brush against the alarm clock by my bedside, blindly trying to find the snooze button.

Once they succeed in their mission, my arm falls slack again off the side of my bed. "What the hell?" I say out loud but mostly to myself. I kept having weird dreams on random nights and could never decipher the meaning of them. My head throbbed, and I immediately knew that the effects of my insomnia would be a bitch today.

My phone rings which causes me to wince in pain at the loud noise directly by my ear on the pillow. I hurry up and answer it without looking at the screen.

"What?" I hiss out, not trying to sound annoyed but I can't help it.

"Looks like sleeping beauty's up from her beauty nap," I hear someone laugh on the other end of the phone.

"What do you want Sai?" I retort, not in the mood for his games right now.

"Well, since you're finally up with the rest of the population, me and Ant wanted to go throw the ball around at the field, and I'd figured I'd try to call. Ant said it was a lost cause, but I had faith. You down?"

I pinch the bridge of my nose and breathe out. "What time is it?"

"7:00am bro. We wanted an early start before the event tonight."

"I'll come, just give me a minute."

"Perfect, we're pulling into your driveway now, see you in 60 seconds." Click.

I pull a pillow over my face to block out the rising sun rays seeping through the blinds in my room. Even though I just woke up, I feel exhausted as hell like I hadn't slept in weeks. I reach over to my bedside table and feel around for a 5-hour energy. I usually keep them there for times like this, when I need an extra kick to get me through the day. I find it then bring it to my lips as I slowly remove the pillow and open my eyes, adjusting to the light.

After gulping down the 5 hour, I hear activity downstairs in my house, and I know that Ant and Sai let themselves in, like always. I throw the pillow back over my face, silently willing them to change their minds and go back to the car. Why did I agree to this?

I hear footsteps bounding up the stairs and audibly groan, knowing they're about to give me shit. They burst in my room and I brace myself for what's about to happen.

"Get your ass up Woods," I hear Saiyr say as he saunters over to my bed. I assume he saunters because I can't see him, but I hear his voice get closer with every word.

"You've got to stop doing this Kai," I hear Anthony say as he stands leaning on the door. Again, that was an assumption because I still haven't turned to look at them. I just know my friends well enough to know their every antic.

"You act like I can control what's happening to me," I say but my words sound muffled under the pillow. My comfort is yanked off my face by Saiyr, sucker punching me with the light. I rush to put my arm over my eyes. I have a vague sense of Deja-vu, but I can't grasp the image that flickers in my mind.

"Hurry up before the field gets packed Woods. We need to make sure that throwing arm of yours is good to go by the time the season starts," Ant says as he pushes off the door frame and heads to my closet.

He comes out a second later, tossing my gym bag onto the foot of my bed causing my cleats to hit my shin and a small burst of pain to shoot up my leg. This causes me to wake up fully.

"Alright alright, I'm getting up," I slowly rise and toss the blanket off me. I blink up at Anthony towering over me and look over to see Saiyr sitting at my desk, flipping through a magazine I had laying there.

I stand up and Ant takes a step back, patting my shoulder a little too firmly as if pushing me towards the bathroom.

"You're in dire need of a shower bro," Saiyr says covering his nose with his finger but not looking up from the magazine. I now see it's my OG Playboy edition from 1999 with Naomi Campbell on the front.

"And you're in dire need of a facial reconstruction but I don't say anything."

I walk into the bathroom and close the door, lowering the volume to his laughter. I lean over the sink and look at myself in the mirror. "Wow, you look like shit," I quietly say, and start the water so I can brush my teeth.

After doing my routine, I hop in the shower, even though I'm about to go sweat and have to do this all over again.

Once I'm dressed, I meet them downstairs in the kitchen and grab a granny smith apple from the fruit bowl in the middle of the breakfast table.

"You ready?" I ask lifting an eyebrow at them standing by the front door.

"Funny, get your ass in the car," Ant says.

After tossing the football around for a couple of hours, and going through a few drills, we lay out on the grass, exhausted, watching the clouds slide around in the sky.

"You figure out what you're going to say at the event tonight yet?" Anthony asks me, still entranced by the clouds. I let the question linger in the air for a little second before responding. "I kind of have a general idea, but I keep feeling like it's missing something."

Tonight, was my mom's book release party for her newest release titled *Where to Now*. It's one of the most highly anticipated releases of the year and is sure to become a New York Times Bestseller by the end of the week.

I'm supposed to be giving a little speech and introducing her to speak and answer questions to multiple execs and longtime fans who oversaw her popular fan pages. Pressure doesn't even begin to describe what I've been feeling lately, which probably explains why my insomnia has kicked back in at full force.

"I don't know why you didn't just ask me to write it for you. I'm a beast at coming up with shit to say on the spot," Saiyr says, and I can hear the smile in his voice.

"So, we're just going to act like your speech at the championship party last year was Oscar worthy?" I laugh in reply.

"That one doesn't count, I was drunk and barely coherent to what was actually happening."

"Who's to say you won't be a drunk fool tonight either," Anthony questions him.

"Wow, what do you take me for?" he gasps in mock horror, "I won't get drunk until the after party tonight, I mean I do have *some* morals Davidson."

We hear some giggles off to our right and I lift my head up a little to see what the commotion was.

"And here come the things that test those morals," Saiyr growls like a lion who's just found their prey.

"Calm your tits Jacobs, I'm sure they wouldn't want you drooling all over their polished shoes," I retort.

I recognized the girls that piled onto the field as the cheerleading team at my school. We were juniors at San Diego State University, so we played for the Aztecs. The cheerleaders weren't supposed to be practicing today, but I guess they felt they needed to make sure everyone was in sync and ready to go for the first game coming up soon.

One of them winks at me and I recognize her as this girl named Tracey that's in my literature research class. I roll my eyes and put my head back down on the grass.

"Alright boys, watch and learn." Saiyr stands up and brushes off his pants, then rubs at his hair to get the grass out. Me and Ant raise up to sit with our arms rested behind our backs, giving us a perfect view of the group of girls stretching each other out across the field in front of us.

He walks up to the new captain, Britney, then bows like she was the Queen of England or something. I shake my head at him and watch her laugh at what he's doing.

Sometimes I'm surprised at the number of girls he pulls with his corny pick-up lines. I always tell him they only put up with him because of his hazel colored eyes.

He kisses her hand and I swear I can see a blush on her face from here. The other cheerleader girls snicker to themselves, causing Anthony and I to look at each other with the "is he really pulling this off?" look.

She gives him her phone, I'm assuming to put his number in, because I see him start to make a phone call. He turns to look at us with a wicked grin and Britney's phone pressed to his ear. I hear his phone go off in the bag next to me and reluctantly go to answer it knowing he's about to make a show of this.

I look at his phone screen and see an unknown number on the caller ID. I answer and put it to my ear without saying anything, looking at him in his eyes.

"What was that you said about her not wanting me?" he winks at me.

"I'm sure she wouldn't after she finds out your dick is broken and can't get up even if held at gun point," I wink back, and he just laughs then hangs up.

He gives her back her phone then says something that makes her laugh. After he's done swooning her, he waves at the other cheerleaders, and starts walking back over to us.

"Take notes boys, I just got a date to the event tonight."

"You're bringing a random chick to Mrs. W's important event?" Anthony says standing up and collecting his bag from the grass beside him.

"She's not random bro, I know her." Saiyr grabs his bag and tosses It over his shoulder.

"Oh yea? What's her name?"

"Braylin, Bianca something, I forgot, but it doesn't matter." He repositions his bag so that it's draped across his chest like a crossbody. "Look, all she needs to know is my name so she can scream it all night tonight."

We all walk to Anthony's red convertible Mercedes C-class, and Saiyr hops in the back without waiting for the door to be unlocked.

"If you bust up my car, I'm busting your knee and you'll be out the whole season," Ant says to him as he slides in the driver's seat.

"Look at you boys, all spiffy and crisp looking. You ready for your speech son?" My dad says as we walk up to greet him on the curb. I had him meet us outside of the event venue at the valet booth.

Saiyr, Anthony and I, all got ready at Anthony's house after stopping by mine so I could shower again and grab my suit for tonight.

"Of course, Mr. C, our Malakai is always prepared," Saiyr winks at me while patting both of his hands on my shoulders while standing beside me. "If you'll excuse me, I see my lovely date for the evening inside looking delectable."

His eyes widen when he realizes who he's talking too, "I mean divine." He hurries inside before my dad can reply to his slip up.

"Remind me again why we're friends with him?" Anthony whispers in my ear. I give a slight chuckle, unable to fully laugh because my nerves are getting the best of me. "Mr. C, always a pleasure," Anthony nods at my dad then shakes his hand firmly and heads in.

"Those boys are something else, aren't they?" I just nod in response, unable to fully focus on the man in front of me. "What's going on with you son?"

I snap out of the momentary daydream I slipped into and just shake my head, "It's nothing dad, just nerves, that's all."

He gives me a once over then shakes his head. "Follow me."

He leads me inside the venue to a vacant room down a dimly lit hall. It was the venue owner's main office and was filled with multiple bookshelves of books and little historical trinkets.

"Alright, tell me what's going on." He leans against the desk in the middle of the room with his hands resting in his pants pockets.

I walk past him to look out the windows behind the desk. They were facing the parking lot out front and gave a perfect view of the people waiting for the valet to park their cars.

"It's just-," I begin to say then stop. Dad waits for me to continue, giving me the time I need to gather my thoughts. "I just want to say the perfect words and not mess up her big night, because it's really important to her. I want them all to know exactly how good of a person she is and how important her work is to the world."

I turn from the window and face him, hoping not to see a disappointing look in his eyes. I'm relieved when I see him smiling at me, then get a little annoyed.

"I'm serious dad, I know it might not be that big of a deal to some, but it's a big deal to me."

"I know son, it just warms my heart to see the love you have for your mom. I could only hope you feel the same way about me."

"Dad," I groan out, not really in a joking mood.

"Okay Okay," he puts his hands up in defense, "But seriously, don't think too much about it. Anything you say about your mom will come from the heart and will mean the world to her. It's clear as day what your mom means to you and that will be conveyed through your eyes. Don't sweat the words too much and just say exactly what's on your heart." He takes one hand out, waving it in the air dismissively like the answer to my problems were straightforward.

I shake my head and give him a half smile. "Why do you make everything sound so much simpler?"

He walks over and hooks his arm behind my neck like he was giving me a noogie. "Because I'm a cool dad."

I escape from his grasp and he lets out a soft laugh. "You're not that cool," I mumble as I straighten my suit jacket.

"You're right, but I do have an even cooler son who helps me to see the positive in every situation, even when he can't see it himself." He starts walking towards the door.

"Well, let me go make sure your mother isn't a nervous wreck like her son. I love you, you'll do amazing."

With that statement, he walks out the door and leaves me to stand and think more on what he said. After a few deep breathes and whispering encouraging movie quotes to myself, I head out towards the back of the building where the event is taking place.

As I walk in, I see it's packed with rows of seats, and cameras sit at the back of the room angled toward the elevated stage upfront. I spot Saiyr, Anthony and the cheerleading captain, Britney, sitting up front. They're engaged in what looks like an amusing debate, but I don't have time to stop and chat. I want to see my mom before everything starts, so I head towards the stairs that lead to the backstage.

Once I'm backstage, I see multiple people running back and forth preparing for the event.

It's set up to be like a recorded book club with a question and answer session, that'll go up on all streaming and social media platforms. I spot my mom sitting in a makeup chair while a makeup artist taps a brush into some powder then swipes it across her face.

My dad stands next to her, both parents engaged in their conversation, laughing and smiling about something.

Seeing them together always gets me excited about the idea of finding my wife one day. Too bad it's not going to be anytime soon. Girls these days only want to be with me because of my status and the fact that I might go pro one day, so I'm a walking money sign to them.

On top of that, I need to get my life in order before I allow someone into my life again.

I walk over to my parents and it's like my mom could sense my presence because she immediately looks in my direction.

"Malakai! You made it! I was afraid you'd gotten lost and couldn't find the building." The makeup artist stops applying the powder and my mom hops out the seat.

She gathers me into a big warm hug and kisses my cheek, then grabs a wipe from the makeup artists' station and wipes the lipstick stain that was left behind. "Hey Ma," I say giving a shy smile, "You ready for tonight?"

"I am now that you're here," she smiles and cups both of my cheeks in her hands.

"I'm proud of you Ma. You're dream of becoming a famous author came true."

"I couldn't have done it without you, you know that." She hugs me again then holds me out at arm's length, giving me a once over then a quizzical look. "Are you trying to steal all of my spotlight? The cameras are going to forget about me and put all their focus on you."

"I told him that when he tried the suit on at the tailors," my Dad said walking up and sliding his arm around my mom's waist.

I shake my head and before I can respond, someone who's working the event walks up and says, "Mrs. Woods, we go on in 5 minutes, if you could make your way towards the stage please," then runs off in the other direction.

"Well, that's my cue loves, see you on the other side," she kisses my dad then gives me one last hug before heading to the front of the stage and sitting on the red cushioned chair.

They had the stage set up like it was the Oprah Winfrey talk show and I admired the whole set up. My dad and I watch from backstage as they begin the countdown until the start of the event and yell action.

The crowd gives a round of applause and then the host begins her introduction. The event moves on smoothly and my mom answers questions from the audience, then reads an excerpt from her book which sparks a discussion with her and the host about the struggles of finding your purpose in the world today.

I paid attention for the most part, but as it got closer to the time for me to say my speech, my nerves shot up to an all-time high. "Now we have a special word from Mrs. Wood's son, Malakai Woods, quarterback of the San Diego state Aztecs!"

On cue I walk out to the front of the stage and wave to the crowd as I stand at the podium to the right of the couch set up. I hear Saiyr and Anthony barking like dogs and cheering me on. Once the applause dies down, I begin my speech.

"Good Evening everyone. I struggled so much with finding the right words to say about my mother tonight, not because I couldn't think of anything, but because I thought of everything." I look around the crowd and make eye contact with Saiyr and he shoots me a thumbs up.

"I thought of everything she's done for me over the years, and everything she means to me. I thought of how, when I was younger, she showed me that my words are powerful and will always make an impact no matter how little or unimportant *I* think they are."

I look at my mom and see her eyes start to glisten with unshed tears. "She showed me that no matter what obstacle is thrown in your path, you can always overcome it, not by merely stepping over, but she said I needed to bulldoze my way through it and make sure there's no life left in it."

My mom laughs along with the crowd. I look past her to where my dad is standing off to the side of the stage in perfect view of me.

"I know that with her words and her work, she has impacted and is able to impact so many lives, and help people through the rough times and remind them, 'it's okay to slow down and breathe, as long as with that next breath you come out more determined than before'. I love you mom and want you to know that you deserve this more than anyone."

Someone brings out a trophy and hands it to me. "I would like to present you with the Bailey's Women's Prize for Fiction." The audience erupts into applause and my mom's mouth drops open in shock.

She puts her hand to her chest and rises from her seat to come towards me. I hand her the award and kiss her cheek, "Surprise Mom."

"How'd you keep this from me?"

"They emailed Dad saying they wanted to honor you and dad asked if we could pull this little surprise on you and they were all for it." She turns towards dad across the stage and blows him a kiss and he winks in response.

"Congratulations Mom." I give her a hug then walk off the stage to sit next to Anthony in the front row.

"Another shot bartender!" Saiyr yells to a kid standing by the punch bowl at the party.

"It's your turn to carry him out to the car," Anthony says to me as we watch him standing on top of a coffee table dancing to the music blasting from the speakers.

He had a solo cup in his right hand, and his left hand was firmly secured on Britney's waist as she was bent over twerking on him. "How are they both even on that table right now?" I ask Anthony, genuinely confused.

"Hey Malakai," a voice says to me from behind. I turn around to see Tracey from the cheerleading team looking at me with heavy eyelids. Seems as though someone got some liquid courage to come talk to me.

"Wassup Tracey?"

It's sad to see how desperate females are for attention these days. I know she only wants me because I have a 6 pack and a guaranteed spot on any pro team of my choosing. She doesn't even know me other than the fact that I have a pretty face that is a blessing and a curse.

"Brit told me what you did for your mom, so freakin' sweet of you," she tries to add a sexy breathy tone to her voice, but ends up sounding like she's wheezing and trying to breathe through a bad lung.

"Yep," I reply but look around the room trying to figure when and where Anthony snuck off too. He must've left right when he heard her voice.

Bastard.

"So, listen, my parents are gone for the rest of the night," she shouts over the music and I look back at her, noticing that she's gotten a little closer. She is now so close, that her breasts are almost touching my stomach.

She was shorter than me, probably around 5'5 and I was a big 6'2 with muscles that'll give Michael B. Jordan a run for his money.

"If you want, you can come over and watch a little Netflix. Maybe chill after," she looks up at me while batting her eyelashes and I have to contain the laughter that's trying to escape my mouth.

"Listen, I'm not really interested. You're a cool girl though, I'm just not really feeling..." I move my hand back and forth between us, "This."

Her eyes go wide.

"Oh, did you think I wanted to have sex with you?" She tries to morph her face to reflect something that resembles disgust, but it just shows the sting of rejection. "I just wanted someone to hang out with after the party since I'll be bored. But clearly, all guys think about is the next vagina they can bury themselves into." She snorts while rolling her eyes dramatically.

She looks passed my shoulder at what I'm assuming is another prospect on her list then back at me. "You know what, never mind. If you'll excuse me." She grabs the cup out of a random guys hand next to us and downs its contents in one swift gulp. She shoves the drink into my chest, and I grab it so that it doesn't fall and get crushed by the dancing college students. She brushes past me, towards the direction of her new love interest.

Once she's gone, I blow out the breath I didn't realize I was holding and look to the kitchen, locking eyes with Anthony. He walks back over and places his hand on my shoulder.

"Sorry to leave you hangin' bro, but *that* was one train wreck I was looking to avoid." We both laugh and go back to enjoying the party, talking to our other friends and students that go to our school.

That night I get home at 3:00 am and try to go through the front door as quietly as possible, so I don't wake anyone up. I'm sure they already heard the alarm system beep, but I still wanted to be cautious.

My mom had a big night and she was tired at dinner when we went out to celebrate after the event. I head towards the stairs and walk up them slowly, so they don't creek under my weight.

Once safely in my room, I close the door behind me and plop on my bed. The only light on in here was coming from the lamp on my nightstand, which caused a nice subtle ambience to flood the room.

After a beat, I look to turn my nightstand light off and attempt to force myself to go to sleep. Now that I wasn't stressing as much anymore, maybe my body will start acting right again.

I notice a piece of paper on the nightstand and pick it up to read it.

PROUD OF YOU SON. YOU WILL DO AMAZING THINGS IN LIFE. (IF YOU COULD LEARN TO THROW A FOOTBALL RIGHT THAT IS) ;).

LOVE DAD.

Hearing my dad say things like this always had me feeling warm and happy on the inside, so why does reading it now make me feel uneasy?

I put the paper back down on the nightstand and turn off the light. Once I close my eyes, the feeling of sleep begins to creep up on me, and I'm grateful tonight I'll be able to get probably the best sleep I've had in a long time.

Imani Lewis

Thank you so much for reading and I would greatly appreciate it if you left an honest review! I had fun writing Hendrix and Ariana's story and hoped you enjoyed reading it. It was so different than what I'm used to writing and was really a splurge piece that turned into something more.

I love each and every one of you and hope you stay amazing.

If you'd love to discuss with me books that I've written or anything at all, join my facebook reader group through my author facebook page.

Imani Lewis